A TIME IN TEXAS

A Western Fiction Novel

By

ALEX ALEXANDER

This novel is a work of fiction. All characters and events portrayed in this book have been created by the author's imagination and refer no person living or deceased.

A TIME IN TEXAS

Copyright 2008 by Alex Alexander

ISBN: 9781467940337

Alex Alexander is a sixth generation Texan. Most of his life has been spent on a ranch in Central Texas. On the down side of seventy he and his wife of fifty six years are few of the old timers still trying to hang on to the only way of life they have ever known. Working cattle and breaking horses seems to have gone the way of the dinosaurs, but there is still some of the old die hards still around.

Other Books by Alex Alexander

Once a Ranger Always a Ranger

Finders Keepers

Sandstone

Trouble in San Juan County

A Time in Texas (Reprint)

Dedication

In memory of Elmer Kelton

Chapter One   *

The funeral procession stopped at the top of the hill, and all of the friends of Elsie Adams gathered around the open grave site. The pallbearers placed the oak casket on the two pipes that lay crossways on the grave. Elsie's brother, a Baptist Minister from Ballinger, cleared his throat and asked for a quiet moment of prayer. "Heavenly Father as we commit Elsie Adams to this good earth we ask you to take her in Your arms and welcome her home.

"We pray Your hand of comfort and the understanding of Your love will be upon her family and friends, amen." The Minister spoke of the childhood of his sister and himself, and of their commitment to God. He told of her love for Ben Adams, her husband, and three children. He spoke of dedication to her church, work for the community, and above all her faith in her Heavenly Father. In closing the Minister quoted the Twenty Third Psalm and asked all to bow and say the Lord's Prayer with him. The pallbearers set the ropes under the casket and raised it slightly as the pipes were removed. Then they lowered Elsie into her resting place in the good earth that was created by The Maker of all things both great and small.

All that were gathered walked the short distance from the family cemetery to the old ranch house surrounded by huge oak trees. The ladies of the First Baptist Church of San Angelo had spread a luncheon that would feed twice as many people. Several tables were covered with all kinds of dishes. After the meal was finished the crowd started to depart one by one. All of them spoke to each member of the family, telling them how much they loved Elsie and if they could help in any way please let them know.

Just before sunset Ben and his son James walked down to the grave site. The last rays of the sun filtered through the giant oak trees that grew around the wrought iron fenced family cemetery. Texas Blue Bonnets and Indian Paint Brushes along with the Sweet Williams were in all their beauty and it was a very peaceful scene.

The fresh mound of earth covering Elise's grave was covered with all of the different flowers and wreaths sent by friends. Ben and James stood quietly with hats off and heads bowed for a time. Then James placed his hand on his dad's shoulder and said, "Ben, mom is in a far better place and her suffering is over. I love her as much as you, but we must continue on as she would have us do."

His dad replied, "Son, she was the most precious thing that ever happened to me."

"James, let me show your lineage. I know you have visited here a few times, but I am going to leave the ranch to you when I am placed there by your mother. I pray you will treat this place as all of us have and you can pass it on to your son."

At the south end of the cemetery, at the west fence there was four granite grave markers. Each one was a double headstone where the names of man and wife were cut into the stones. These all faced to the east. The first stone was that of Ben's great great grandfather Benjamin Adams, 1800-1860 his wife Lucy Adams1802-1863. "James, this man was my great great granddad. He came from Ireland to Tennessee then to Texas. He fought with Sam Houston in the war for the freedom we have today. For his service to the Republic, he was awarded part of this range. That old stone wall you see by that big live oak was where his home stood."

The next stone bore the name of James Adams 1831-1890 and Sara Adams, 1829-1896. "This is the man I named you after son. He served with the Texas Rangers in the Indian troubles. He added a few sections of land to the ranch and started a breeding program to produce a better grade of

2

livestock."

The next stone was that of Ben's father and mother. Travis Adams 1863 - 1925 and Mary Adams 1865 - 1928.

"James, I know you loved him as I love you and I have tried to make this ranch into something you will be proud of after I join your mother. You have the strength and education to do the same for your son. I will have provided for your sisters in like funds because they are more inclined to the big city life."

James replied, "Dad, I will do my best, but you are a long way from needing my help just yet. I need to tell you a few things first in confidence. Let's go sit on the porch for awhile." They walked back to the ranch house and sat in a couple of rocking chairs at the far south end of the porch.

Just as they were seated, Maude Lange who was Ben's older sister, handed them a cup of coffee. Maude's husband was killed in World War One. They had no children, and when Elsie became ill Maude came to help Ben take care of her. Ben had asked her to just move in with them as she had no family. They thanked her for the coffee and she retreated into the house. Ben asked, "Son, what is it you wanted to tell me that is so important?"

"Dad, there is a lot I need to tell; first I have asked a young lady to marry me. Her name is Ruth Pearson. She was raised by her aunt and uncle; her parents were both killed in a car wreck. I met her in college and she is very mature. I know you will like her and mother would have loved her. We plan to get married in June here at the ranch if it is okay with you."

A grin was on Ben's face as he hugged and told him, "James, if you want me to keep that quiet, you're going to have to hog tie and gag me. This makes me so happy. I think it's wonderful."

James said, "Dad, I thank you for your blessing, but

that is not what I want you to keep to yourself. As you know my major in college was Government. After graduation I was interviewed by a group from the Army Air Corps. Since I already have a pilot's license, they offered me a commission to work in the Air Corps Information Gathering Division. It will be a six year commitment. Should I stay in for twenty years I can receive full retirement.

"That's still not what I want you to keep under your hat. As I was in the meeting they explained about the war in Europe and said America would be drawn into the conflict by Germany or Japan by1940 or 1941.When this happens almost everything will be rationed.

"Before this happens, you need to have a good stock of whatever it takes to keep the ranch in operation. From what I heard this is going to be a long hard war, perhaps up to six years. We as a nation are ill equipped. The demand for men and raw materials will be a tremendous strain on all Americans, until it is over. I was not told to keep it quiet but I think it best to not mention it to anyone, not even your best friends. If the word gets out it would cause a panic."

Ben agreed with his Son and it gave him a lot to think about. The next morning James's twin sisters returned to college.

Arlene and Marlene were enrolled in Baylor University in Waco.

James and Ruth were married that happy day in June. The ceremony was performed by Amos Brown the local minister who had baptized Ben, Elsie and their three children. Maude was present as was Pepe Rojas, his wife Eva and, son Joaquin. Pepe had worked for Ben for several years and after Joaquin finished high school he also joined the work force. The Rojas family was like family to the Adams. Joaquin and James were the same age and grew up together.

After the bride was kissed by Ben, hugged by Maude

"Auntie," Ruth replied, "James is my husband and I trust him to know what's best for both of us. I dread for this war to be upon us but it is something we can't hide from. There is nothing I would love better than for us to remain here as we are. If James enlists now and there is no war for America then James has given six years of his life to his country. If there is a war he will not have the opportunity to choose as he does now. From what I have gathered in college, and the way Germany and Japan are trying to dominate the world, I think that there is no way America can stay neutral."

"James," Ben said, "I think I know how you feel and it is your decision to do what you think is best for you and Ruth. If we are pulled into a worldwide conflict I would want you to be in the best position possible to do your best for your country."

Maude added, "James always does his best at anything he does, you know that Ben. I just hate to see he and Ruth leave us. These two precious children are so dear to me that I will feel lost. I know James will excel in his job for his country." The next morning James called and told Major Lee that he would accept the opportunity that was offered to him, and was grateful that he could be of service to his country. The Major told James to report to his office at Lackland Air Base at ten a. m. on the first day of August. James would be sworn in and receive his orders and housing assignment. The next day he would be issued his uniforms and be given a tour of the base. After that it would be classes and training.

James explained to the family his instructions, and said the ranch work should go on as usual until next to the last day of July. Ben told Pepe, Eva and Joaquin of James going into the Air Force and Joaquin asked if he could go with him. Eva said, "No! No! No! You need to stay with Mama and help your Papa and Mr. Ben. These two old men can't do all

7

this work by themselves. Beside, your girl friend, Maria Murillo, won't let you even go to town on Saturdays without her being with you. Sometimes I think she has you wrapped around her little finger."

Ben and Pepe had a good laugh at Joaquin's expense. Joaquin looked at Pepe and said, "I know now who wears the pants in our family." At that sharp remark Eva and Ben got the laugh on Pepe.

The next weeks passed swiftly, as the work progressed. James told Ben he should build a couple of two room houses over close to where Pepe's home was, and hire two more good hands.

James spoke, "Dad, by next spring all of the fence lines need to be cleared again of the brush. You and Pepe will have more work than you can handle, even with the seasonal men you hire to do the farming for the spring and fall crops. You and Pepe need to let Joaquin handle all of the hay hauling and storage.

"I'm not saying you two are getting to old to do the hard work. You need to understand that with sixty-two sections of land and all of the cattle you are running now you need to spend more time being boss instead of trying to be just another hired hand. Pepe knows how to run this ranch and what it takes to make sure it's run right. I know Aunt Maude worked as an accountant for twenty years. You need to let her set up a complete set of books as she needs something to make her feel as though she is needed here and is earning her keep. You need to pay her a salary just as you do everyone else."

Ben had that big grin on his face again and said, "James, I know right now you are going to run this place better than I ever will. I don't think your college degree has put these thoughts in your head, I just think you are a realist and a natural born rancher. I hope and pray you and Ruth have a son that inherits all of the good qualities you two have."

After supper Ben sat at the kitchen table with Maude while they had a last cup of coffee. Ben said, "Maude, you sure make good coffee. You have gotten me spoiled on your cooking too, and I need to ask a favor of you."

Maude replied, "If you want me to bake you a batch of sourdough biscuits all you have to do is say so. I know how much you liked the ones mother made when we were kids."

"No sister, I need some help in the worst way. I need you to start keeping a complete set of books on the operation of the ranch, of every penny we make and every one we spend. I've made a mess of it since Elsie passed away. I hate to place this responsibility on you, but I know you are very capable to handle it. You can pay yourself whatever you would charge anyone else."

"Ben, after we lost Elsie I have had the feeling of being a burden on you. I would be very happy to help you any way I can; you know that Ben. Give me the key to the office and I can start now."

"Sister, you can start in the morning, the job will be there waiting for you. I don't want you to lock yourself in the office and try to do this in one day."

Maude came out of her chair, walked over to Ben and gave him a hug, kissed his cheek and said, "Ben, you don't know how happy it makes me to be needed by someone."

Chapter Three

July the Fourth was celebrated with a rodeo in Angelo, with Joaquin winning the bull dogging contest. After the close of the festival they all went to Pepe and Eva's to enjoy the goat Pepe had barbequed. James and Joaquin cranked up a gallon and a half of homemade ice cream that was mixed up by Maude. While the ladies went into the house, the men sat on the front porch to talk. Ben explained to Pepe and Joaquin of the things that James had mentioned. He asked them if they knew a couple of good hands they could hire. Joaquin asked did he want single or married men. Ben asked Pepe his opinion and he said he thought married men may be more reliable, but with single men they could build one house, kind of like a bunkhouse. Just build it large enough to house the extra men they needed to work at roundup and branding time.

Pepe explained that Eva could cook for the two permanent hands. Then they could hire a cook for the time of roundup. Ben told Joaquin and Pepe to start looking for two good all around cowboys that could work out of the saddle as well as in it. They could furnish their own saddles and pick out their own string out of our horses. Ben said he would get started on the bunkhouse in the morning. After they left Pepe's, and got home, James told his dad that he didn't even want him to think about building anything. "Just get in your pickup and go to town. Stop at Higginbottom's Lumber Company and tell them to give you a price on what you want built. They can build it before you could get all of the material to the job site. You might think you can save a few bucks by doing the labor ourselves, but what happens to the rest of the work you really know how to do?"

"James, you are right as rain and I can think of a thousand things I need to take care of. Will you go with me in the morning?"

James replied, "I'll go and I'll drive. I want to make sure we get there." Ben knew James was ribbing him from the sly little grin on his face.

July was in its last three days as the two new cowboys dropped their war bags on the floor of the new eight man bunk house. These two were good solid men that Pepe had hired. Ben knew each of them as they had helped in previous roundups. Ben told Pepe that tomorrow night for all of them to come to the ranch house. They were giving James and Ruth a going away supper, and they wanted them to be there to wish the couple a safe and happy venture.

The next morning James and Ruth loaded their belongings into their 1938 Chevy. They then said their goodbyes to Ben and Maude to depart for San Antonio. The young couple wanted to be in San Antonio and spend the night in the Menger Hotel before reporting in at Lackland. Ben and Maude stood on the porch as the car passed over the ridge and was out of site. Tears flowed as Maude stared at the vanishing auto and said to Ben, "I feel like part of my life has left me. I love those children so much. It is hard for me to understand why God lets things like this war in other countries take our children from us."

"Sister, who are we to question what God lets happen in the world. James is a more mature man than I am in some respects. He is doing what he thinks is the right thing to do. I know how the first war took away your husband, and the grief you have suffered. God has His reasons for all things. All we mortals can do is just keep on keeping on."

"I know this is true, but it still leaves an aching in my heart. I know James will write and call us and so will Ruth, but you can't hug a letter or a phone call," Maude said as she squeezed her brother's hand. "Ben, you and your children are all I have left in this world."

James and Ruth were welcomed by Major Lee and his staff and James was quickly settled into the routine of becoming a ninety day wonder of military life. With his R.O.T.C. training at Texas A&M, he quickly adapted. Ruth became acquainted with the other officer's wives, which helped to keep a busy daily routine.

The days turned to weeks and the weeks to months. James and Ruth spent the Thanksgiving Holidays at the ranch. Maude and Eva had prepared a feast that the Pilgrims would have been jealous of. The two Mexican cowboys were dressed in their Sunday best, and were at ease as was Joaquin. It was not only a feast to be thankful for, but a time to renew family relations. The minister, the aging Brother Amos Brown, who had married James and Ruth, offered grace for the meal.

The weather was cold for November, and Ben had a roaring fire going in the fireplace. After Pepe, his family and the cowboys left, the others moved chairs close to the warm fireplace.

Maude was full of questions about Ruth's new life as an officer's wife. Ruth explained base activities that managed to keep the wives occupied most of the time. The only thing that was hard to get used to was the bugle call and the noise from the constant roar of aircraft engines.

Ruth also spoke of the church services that were offered to any denomination. The Major attended the Protestant services with her and James. Ruth said the Major's wife had taken her under her wing, and was a great help in showing her the ropes of military life. Ruth said, "Without Mrs. Lee's help I would have never made it to first base."

Brother Amos Brown asked James if he would mind taking him back to the parsonage. Ben replied, "Are you tired of our company already preacher?"

Amos said, "Ben, you know better than that. I feel

more at home here than anywhere I have visited. I just need to make a call on a couple of old maids that have stuck their nose into something they shouldn't have. I must, as you would say, close the gate before the cows get out."

Amos and James got their coats on and Ben walked with them to the car and shook hands with Amos. He told him that the Adams family would see him at church Sunday morning.

Amos asked James, "Well James, how do you like life in the military?"

"Preacher, I would love to be home helping dad. That is where my heart is. Like I told dad, if we get drawn into this war like the press is saying I would be drafted into the army, navy or marines as a buck private. Not that I wouldn't do my job where ever I would wind up. It's that I can do my country a better job where I am now and it's a lot easier on Ruth.

"I will be transferred to D. C. sometime after the first of the year to go to Intelligence School. I must be qualified to fly and photograph and to report any and all different weapon systems and troop movement. Flying the aircraft is a breeze, but I've got a lot to learn about the rest of it."

James let Amos off at the church parsonage and returned to the ranch. The ladies were in the kitchen cleaning up and Ben was sitting in his easy chair just staring at the fire when James entered the living room. Ben asked, "Well, did you get Brother Amos delivered?"

James replied, "Yes dad I did. God made one of a kind when He made Amos. He is one of the best men I have the good luck to be around."

"Yes son, Amos has been with our church for a long time. I don't think he will quit preaching for our church until he passes on to a better place."

"Dad, I think we better talk about some of the things I told you to keep under your hat. Just before you start spring planting you need to get two five hundred gallon tanks on a stand about six feet tall; one for diesel and one for gasoline. I know we don't have any equipment now that uses diesel but I think you need to purchase a large diesel tractor and two, two ton flat bed trucks. You also need two goose neck trailers that will haul at least a dozen cows or horses. You can move more stock at less cost and diesel will be cheaper than gas. The trucks will outlast a dozen three quarter or one ton gas pickups. Be sure and not let your fuel tanks get below half. You need to keep a couple sets of tires and tubes for each vehicle.

"Don't buy them all at one time and from the same place. When you and Aunt Maude drive over to Waco to visit Arlene and Marlene, buy some there and buy oil by the case. Just pick a case here and there at different times. You have plenty of storage for these things and I know you will need all of it before this conflict is over."

Ben gave James a very serious look and said, "James, you talk like the war has already started."

"Dad, I'm not trying to scare you. What I'm telling is going to happen. F.D.R. can't stop it. England and France are just about on their knees to Hitler trying to stop the German war machine. The more they take the more they want. Japan has run over everything in their path and is just getting started. Before this war ends it will make World War One look like a cake walk.

"There are shipments of arms, aircraft and medical supplies being stocked now to be ready to ship to England at a moment's notice. The majority of the politicians are afraid if they face the fact of this conflict and support the president they would never get reelected. The president is working behind closed doors to get as prepared as he can without ruffling the fat cats feathers in Congress." There are a few people in our political system that face the facts just like you have here.

"Dad, you dug a cellar in case of a tornado outbreak and we have used it several times. That was foresight. That's what the president is doing. I am going to be reassigned to D. C. sometime after the first of the year. Ruth and I will be here for Christmas, and I would like for Major Lee and his wife to come with us if you don't mind. I hope Amos can come too."

"Son, you bring your Major on and I'll make sure Amos is here."

Chapter Four

Late Christmas Eve morning found James, Major Lee and their wives in San Angelo having lunch at The Texas restaurant on Chadbourn Street. Mrs. Lee said that they should not arrive at lunch time without prior notice. James thought it would not make a bit of difference to Ben or Maude, but he just kept quiet. They arrived at the ranch house around two that afternoon. As they stepped out of the car, Mrs. Lee said, "My goodness, I've never looked at such a perfect home in a more perfect location."

Ben and Maude met them at the front door. Hugs, handshakes, with tears and introductions were made as they entered. In the living room by the fireplace, curled up in Ben's easy chair was Brother Amos Brown. Ruth gave Amos a hug and a kiss on the cheek and introduced him to Mrs. Lee and the Major. James put a bear hug on the aging Minister and asked, "Amos have you been keeping Ben out of trouble?"

Amos looked at Ben and told James, "The Good Lord shakes His head every time I try to straighten Ben out. The Lord knows it can't be done."

Ben placed his hand on Amos's shoulder and said, "Amos, if I was any straighter I would have to be a preacher like you instead of an old rancher."

Maude told them both, "You two act like a couple of little boys, each one wanting to be what the other is. You should be thankful that you were born what you are instead of what you act like."

This drew a hardy laugh from all six of them. After Christmas day, Ben and James took the Major on a drive around the ranch. The first stop was to visit with Pepe and Eva. Joaquin and the cowboys were out feeding the live stock and horses. Over Eva's hot coffee, James asked Pepe how things were going. Pepe replied, "I think we have had the best year we have had in a good while. The fall roundup went off without a hitch, and we will send a lot of two year old steers to market this spring. Ben knows more about things than I do. You should be asking him instead of me."

James replied, "Pepe, you are El Segundo, and I want you to keep up with everything that goes with your job. The way Ben and Amos carry on I think I need to rely on your judgment. Sometimes I believe these two old roosters are in their childhood."

Eva said with a grin, "James, you shouldn't be kidding your dad like this. You know Ben knows everything that happens around here. I know you and Amos and Ben kid one another all the time, but Pepe takes everything to serious."

"Eva, I just love to keep dad on his toes, and if I don't I'm scared Amos will get the best of him. I know Pepe is a serious man and a good man and he got the best when he married you. I always feel at home when I am here with you two."

The drive around the pastures had taken up most of the day, and the pastures where no stock grazed were not visited. As they drove by the barns, storage sheds and corrals James noticed the large storage fuel tanks on the elevated stands. In one of the sheds was a new large green diesel tractor.

Chapter Five

Three days after Christmas the two military couples said their goodbyes and left, taking Amos Brown by his home in the church parsonage. Amos said as he stepped out of the car, "I will have all of you in my prayers each day and night, may you have a safe journey home."

Back at the ranch, the big old ranch house seemed so empty and quiet. Maude broke the silence as she spoke to Ben. "Well, guess I had better get back to my work on the books that I am keeping. I don't like much having it up to date. The longer I wait the farther behind I get."

Ben asked, "Sister, how does it look so far? Do we have enough money left to buy groceries?"

"Well, you spent quite a sum on the tractor and the fuel tanks and having them filled up. Unless you have some receipts you haven't given me, I think you could go ahead and get those two trucks James told you about. We would be okay to make another year without selling this falls steers until next spring."

"Maude, you're not pulling my leg are you? This couldn't be something you and Brother Amos cooked up could it? It sounds just about like something that he would hatch up just to boost my spirits a little bit."

"When it comes to my bookkeeping and your money, I don't joke with anyone, more especially you. I can tell that Elsie kept a tight rein on you, and this ranch is one of the best businesses that I have ever kept a set of books for. As long as you give me your paid and charge receipts and income receipts I can tell you any time what your financial status is. I was going to cook you those sourdough biscuits for supper but I've changed my mind."

"Aw Sister, I wasn't harping on you and Amos, and I am sorry if you took it that way. I tell you what, just to show you I was kidding you, I think we should ride into town and eat us a steak supper." Maude smiled and they went.

January, February and March passed as time flies. Things at the ranch never seem to change. Cows and horses, sheep and Angora goats kept the crew busy. Shearing time for the latter two was done by the same families that had done it for as long as Ben could remember. Pepe gave his daily orders to Joaquin and the two cowboys. Spring roundup was ready to start and the bunkhouse was full of part time cowhands and their gear. The old chuck wagon had been put into retirement and a new cook shack with all the modern amenities had been installed.

Electric lights, a butane cook stove, a long eating table with benches on each side that seated twelve, with a set of cabinets complete with a double sink and running hot water. The dishware was still the same old blue porcelain metal. Eva told Ben glass dishes wouldn't last a week with this bunch of rowdy cowboys. She told Ben since the new cook shack had been built that she could handle all of the cooking. She told him that the old cook that had cooked for them in the past had gone to Mexico to live with his daughter. She let Ben know that the old man didn't know how to cook on anything except a wood fire out in the open and didn't want to learn on this new modern stuff. He claimed it would not be sanitary. She would prepare a good sack lunch for each of the cowhands. They could take them as they rode in the pickups to where the horses and branding pen were. Then they could put the sacks in the large ice chests in the pickup beds.

Ben said, "Eva, the old days are gone forever. I'm

thankful Pepe and me got to see those good old days. Lunch sack cowboys; my word what's the world coming to?" Ben was thankful that he had a couple like Pepe and Eva, as these good people were the salt of the earth.

On his way back to the ranch house Ben stopped by the rural mailbox and picked up the last three days mail. He sorted through it trying to see if there might be a letter from James and Ruth. Since his reading glasses were at the house he laid the bundle of mail in the seat and drove on home.

After parking the pickup, he made his way thru the kitchen door and got a whiff of Maude's sourdough biscuits cooking in the oven. He dropped the mail on the kitchen table and called Maude. She answered from the office and told him not to fool around in the kitchen that she had supper almost ready. She didn't need to tell him that, he already knew it.

Maude came to the kitchen with her apron on and Ben's glasses in her hand. "I thought you might pick up the mail today so I brought your glasses. You might see to read if you put them on."

Ben replied, "Sister, I can see real good a little ways off but up close everything is real blurry, it all kinda' runs together."

"Don't you know that's a sure sign that father time is slipping up on you. The next thing you know you'll likely be wearing a pair of bifocals all time."

Ben didn't want to get her started on the conversation of his old age so he put on his glasses and went thru the mail. Most of it was sales of some kind and coupons for a nickel discount on a purchase of over a dollar at the local five and dime store. There were two letters, one from James and one from Ruth. To Ben that was just a waste of an envelope and a three cent stamp. There was two days difference in the dates they were mailed. Ben thought James forgot to tell them something and Ruth was filling in what James left out. Ben told Maude about the letters and she said, "Ben, all you need to do is open and read them. Then you will find what the problem is if there is one."

There was no use in Ben trying to explain what he was trying to tell her. He just shook his head a tiny bit where she couldn't see it and opened the letter from James first. The letter was to Ben and Aunt Maude. It started with hope you are well and things are going good. He asked about Amos, the Rojas family and how the roundup was coming along and things in general. James finally got to the heart of the letter. Ruth had been sick the last few days and is at the base hospital now getting a checkup.

The entire Company under the command of Major Lee was to be transferred to an Army Air Corps base. They were all to undergo extensive training in photography and aerial combat. That was standard procedure for this branch of the service. James explained that as soon as he knew the date they were to pull out he would let them know. In case housing was not available Ruth may have to spend a while at the ranch, if they didn't mind. He said that no one knows just where the new base is but he would let them know as soon as he found out. Well so much for being transferred to D.C.

The letter from Ruth was short and sweet.

Dear Ones:

I have been to the doctor as I have had a sick spell almost every morning for the last two weeks. I want you to know that James Benjamin will arrive in about seven months; he will be called Little Ben. Love to all,

James and Ruth

Ben handed the letter to Maude and just stared at the ceiling. He felt like shouting or maybe he should cry. It was one of the happiest moments of his life. Maude finished the short letter and jumped from her chair. She started hugging Ben and crying at the same time.

Ben said, "Well, it had to happen sooner or later. The baby had better be a boy or they will have to think up another name."

Maude told Ben, "This baby will be a strong healthy boy just like all of you Adams boys have been. I'm going to answer her letter right now. Is there anything you would like me to tell Ruth?"

"Just that the little feller has got to be born in Texas."

Chapter Six

James called Ben the middle of May and told him that everyone has a week's furlough. He said they would see them around noon tomorrow. Ben told James to meet him and Maude at the Texas Cafe and he would buy lunch. James told Ben that they may be a few minutes late, so if they didn't mind waiting they could all order when they arrived. Ben agreed and told his son to drive with care. The next morning Ben picked up the phone and called Amos. "Amos, this is your only friend in the world calling you. I want you to be ready to go to lunch with Maude and me at eleven o'clock, if you can get up that early."

Amos replied, "Ben, you only asked me to go with you because no one else but your sister wants to be seen with you in a public place. I know it may scar my reputation but as a minister of the gospel I feel compelled to go so I can still try to get you over on the sunny side of life. I shall be prepared for your onslaught of my character at eleven sharp. In the meantime I will ask The Lord again for His guidance while in your company."

Ben hung up the phone and told Maude, "Sister, I don't care how nice I try to be to Amos he always gets the best of me."

"Ben, if you two old goats ever get to heaven I hope the Good Lord puts you and Amos in separate pastures with high fences."

Amos told Maude as he climbed into Ben's car, "I hope your ornery brother doesn't expect a poor old preacher like me to fill him up on chicken fried steak, mashed potatoes, cream gravy, pinto beans and a gallon of coffee. I've got just enough to pay for a pack of spearmint gum."

Maude replied, "Amos, if he tries to pass the bill to you I'll take his allowance away from him." Ben sat quietly and acted as if they were not even in the car. He parked in front of the restaurant, walked around the car and opened the doors for Maude and Amos. He removed his hat and made a bow.

Amos asked Maude, "Is Ben sick or just feeling humble? I know that he hasn't asked forgiveness of the way he treats us."

"Amos, in a few minutes you will know why I act this way. Ya'll just get out of the car before people start gawking at you."

They seated themselves at a round table arranged for five people. Ben seated Amos with his back to the front door and sat on one side as Maude sat on the other side of the preacher. The waitress sat three glasses of water before them and asked what they would have to drink with their meal. Maude and Amos ordered sweet tea and Ben asked for coffee, no spoon, no cream, no sugar just coffee.

Ben told the waitress they would like to wait a few minutes before ordering. After a short wait the front door opened as Amos set down his glass of tea. He felt a hand placed on his left shoulder and a kiss brushed his right cheek. As he stood and turned Ruth gave him a hug and said "Surprise." She gave Maude a hug as James had an arm around both Ben and Amos.

After enjoying a good meal, which Ben paid for, they drove to the ranch. Ben said, "Amos, you can spend the night with us and I won't charge you room and board."

"Ben, the last time I stayed the night with you, I got up and slept in the barn. You snored so loud the old rooster started crowing before midnight."

They all gathered on the long porch and sat in the high back rocking chairs that were in a semicircle facing east. There was a cool breeze out of the south bringing the fresh smell of honeysuckle that added to peace and tranquility to the spring afternoon.

Amos said quietly, "I wish the whole world would stay frozen in time just as it is as we sit here enjoying God's handy work. It's a shame that mankind can't live at peace and love one another as God loves man." For a long while no one spoke. The only sounds were those of the gentle breeze in the leaves of the giant oaks and the calling of a mourning dove searching for its mate.

James broke the silence and said, "Amos, in around seven months there will be no peace at this ranch."

"Just what do you mean by that? Do you think this far away war is going to come here to this ranch just to give Ben a little trouble?" Amos asked.

No," replied James, "There is going to be another Ben here to give you more than you can handle."

"Lord help us all, one Ben is more than enough for this entire county. I guess I'd better give up preaching and move off somewhere. If it wasn't for the other good folks around here I'd have already been gone a long time ago."

Ben replied, "Amos, we couldn't run you off with a stick of dynamite, and you know it. If you did try to sneak out of town on a dark night the entire church congregation would have the law arrest you and put you in jail. We would stand out behind the jail in the rain and listen to you preach thru the bars of the cell window."

Ruth spoke quietly, "Amos, I really don't think Little Ben will give you the least bit of blarney that James and Ben kid you with. Little Ben will be easy to love and will not speak an unkind word to you or anyone else. If and when he tries I will give him a lecture that would make his grandfather ashamed."

"You don't mean, or do you, that there is going to be another addition to this wonderful family? I should have known something great was going to happen when Ben asked me to join him and Maude for lunch. He doesn't do a thing like asking me out unless he's got a personal problem. He just wants to rib me just because I'm the only one who puts up with him."

Maude said, "You and Ben carry on worse than two old maids. If anyone besides our family ever listened to you old goats, no one would ever know that you are the best of friends and would gladly give his life to save the other."

"Well, since Ben won't let me move away, I guess I'll just hang on here and baptize my Godson."

James replied, "I need to ask all of you a favor. Since I am going to be transferred to who knows where, I would like for Ruth to stay here with you until Little Ben is born. I hate to be away from her, but there is no choice in the matter. Major Lee advised me that the next few months we're going to be on the move almost constantly. Ruth and I have talked about this at length and she said she would rather be with you folks than anywhere else in the world."

Ben replied, "Son, you know you don't even have to ask. We would love to have Ruth here and you know it. I believe it would maybe keep Amos in a good mood. Lord knows he needs to smile a lot more often than he does."

"Ben, just for saying that, I'll spoil Little Ben so bad that he will not have anything to do with you. I'll even get Maude to help me. Between the two of us you will wish you had of repented years ago. You can bet I'll even get your sister not to bake you any more sourdough biscuits."

"Amos, that's hitting me where it hurts and I ask you to take that back about Maude's biscuits. I know if there is any spoiling to be done I'll do it."

Ben called Pepe and asked he and Eva to join them for supper. Eva told Pepe to ask Ben what she needed to bring. Ben told Pepe to tell her to bring a bunch of sourdough biscuits. Pepe said all she knew how to fix in the way of bread was tortillas and sopapillas. Ben told him to bring the sopapillas.

Ruth and Maude had the meal prepared, and Eva's sopapillas with honey and coffee served as a great dessert.

James asked Pepe if he would take a ride with him around the grazing pastures in the morning. Pepe agreed and said that he would pick him up around six.

Pepe arrived and James waved him to come in. James had three cups of coffee on the table with a plate of Maude's biscuits and a jar of red plum preserves. Ben joined them. The three left the table with all the biscuits, preserves and coffee depleted.

They returned to the ranch house at dusk and James told Pepe thanks for the trip. Ben asked, "What do you think about the pastures? It looks to me like we are in pretty good shape. All we need is a little more rain."

James replied, "Dad, I want you to go to Angelo with me in the morning. I want to visit with a friend that I went to college with. I think that he has some ideas that will improve our pastures and help give us more grazing during dry weather."

The next morning James parked in front of the U.S.D.A. office.

Ben said, "Son, I've never asked the federal government for any help and I'm not going to start now."

"We are not here looking for a handout. Just come inside and try to be civil. The man I'm going to talk to isn't going to stick his nose in your business. I think you might like him if you will just listen to what he has to say."

As they entered two young men were talking. One looked at James and said, "I'll be if it's not my old classmate and best friend, James Adams. I have thought about you often since we finished school."

"Dad, I want you to meet George Pate. He hails from Big Spring. When I found out from Buddy Rose that he was working in this office I wanted you to meet him."

Ben shook hands with a firm grip with George. He told him he was glad to see him being of service to the farmers and ranchers. George asked them to join him in his office and served them coffee. He was a very likeable person and Ben understood James's friendship with him. They chatted about old times at school for a while.

James asked, "George, I hear that you have been working on brush control in this area and I would like to find out more about it. I have noticed that while I have been away that the mesquite, salt cedar, mountain cedar and prickly pear have increased about ten fold. I understand that all of these are taking a lot of moisture from the native grasses. I hope you might give us some information on how to rid the pastures of them."

"I'm happy that you are taking an interest on this problem as you are the first ones that have shown an interest in learning about controlling these plants. They not only take the moisture that starves out the beneficial grasses but also makes it a certain danger to your livestock."

George went into details of the program and said that there was no cost to the rancher for a ten acre demonstration.

"If you are satisfied with the results and want to do the work yourself, all it will cost will be the herbicide that is used, and whatever equipment is required." George gave them the printed brochures with pictures and the results of prior applications. He told them if they wanted to try it to let him know. He would make arrangements and be there with the work crew in a couple of days. He gave them his business card and told James to keep in touch.

Ben didn't say anything as they drove back home. When James parked the car Ben asked, "Why didn't you go ahead and get it setup? I think this might be what we have been needing to do for the last few years. I had no idea that there was a program like this."

James replied, "Dad, all government programs are not trying to tell you how to run your business or trying to get you to become indebted to them. I wanted you to see how this would work for your benefit. If you want to try it just call George and get it set up."

Ben did and it worked. Pepe was given the task of finding someone that could take charge of the operation with the know how to get the job done. As large as the ranch was it took two men and machines to accomplish the full time job.

Chapter Seven

It was a sad goodbye when James departed to return to San Antonio to prepare to be ready for his next assignment. Arrangements were made with what little belongings there were at the base to be shipped to the ranch. Joaquin went with James to drive his car back. Joaquin talked to James at length about service in the military. James told him that when the war broke out there would be a lot of men needed to fight. Joaquin told James that he wanted to go but his mother and girl friend begged him not to.

"Joaquin, you may not have a choice. There is talk of men being drafted into service. You are at the right age to be called up in the first call of duty. If you do have to go, I know you will do your duty because you are one of the best men I know."

On his way back home Joaquin put a lot of thought into what James had told him. The first thing I'm going to do is marry Maria. I will build us a home by mom and dad's house. If I'm drafted my parents can look after Maria, as Ben is watching over Ruth, he thought to himself.

He parked James's car in the shed behind the ranch house and called at the kitchen door. Maude answered and he asked to speak to Ben. Maude told him Ben was at the horse corral. He thanked her and found Ben leaning on the top railing looking at a dozen good cow ponies. Ben asked if everything went ok on the trip and he replied yes, but that he felt kind of lost after he left James at the base. Ben put his arm around Joaquin's shoulder and told him he felt lost too.

Joaquin told Ben of his talk with James and his thoughts of building the house and marrying Maria. He asked Ben for his permission to do so.

Ben said, "Joaquin, you are like a second son to me and I want you to know that when Pepe is too old to run this ranch you are going to be El Segundo. We will start getting your and Maria's home ready to build tomorrow. James taught me how to get things built in a hurry and done right. You just better make sure Maria will say yes or you will be sleeping by yourself. I should have thought about building you a home sometime back, but it's hard for me to think you and James have grown up on me."

"Mr. Ben, I don't know how to thank you. I wish all white people were as good as you and Amos."

"Joaquin I'm not Mr. Ben, just plain old Ben. I know your parents have taught you good and proper manners, but please just call me Ben."

"Yes sir, I'll remember. I want to thank you Ben. This ranch is the only home I've ever known and the only place I ever cared to be. I hope when I die you will bury me in the ranch cemetery."

"Joaquin, you will bury me there way before your time comes. But don't worry about it, I have made sure all of your family will be placed there when the Lord calls their souls home."

Joaquin thought he would wait to tell his parents about what was going to happen. He knew his mother would question him and would want to run things.

The next morning Ben drove into town. Stopping by to get Amos to have breakfast with him, before going to the lumber yard, he banged on the parsonage door and called out.

"Hey you old rascal, I thought you'd be standing out on the curb with your shoes in one hand and your purse in the other just waiting for someone to pick you up for a ride."

"I've changed my mind about you Ben Adams. I thought you'd have more respect for your elders than you do. I can't believe you would treat an old man like you do me. If it would do any good I'd have the ladies bible class pray for you, but I don't want to make the ladies mad at me."

"Well, come on and let's go before they start serving supper instead of breakfast."Amos had slipped out of the back door and was standing beside the pickup. He yelled at Ben, "Are you going to stand and shout at that door all day or do you want me to carry you over here?" Ben couldn't help but grin and told Amos that the Good Lord was going to punish him for making fools of his friends.

At breakfast Ben told Amos about Joaquin and Maria and the home he was going to have built for them. Amos asked if Ben knew when and where they were to be married. Ben said he didn't know but as soon as he found out he would let him know.

After breakfast they went to the lumber yard. They were just opening up as Ben and Amos walked in. Ben told the salesman he wanted to look at some house plans. The salesman asked how large of a house he needed and Ben told him a four or five room house. After looking at the stack of plans, he picked out a five room house with a large bath and asked about the price.

About that time the owner of the business saw Ben and came over to shake his hand. He saw the plan Ben had and asked if he was building a new home for James. Ben told the owner about Joaquin and said the house was for him and his bride. The owner told Ben that he was one in a million that would do that for a hired hand and it showed how good of a man Ben was. He thought about telling Amos what the man said, but he figured Amos would unload both barrels on him, so he just thanked the gentleman instead. Next they went to a well drilling company and Ben asked if they had time to drill a water well for him.

The driller asked Ben, "How many wells have I already drilled on your place, about sixty five?" Ben told him a few more but he needed another one if he could get to it. The crusty old driller told Ben he could start no sooner than now if he knew where to drill. Ben told him about the new home for Joaquin and Maria and when he got his rig to the location that he would be there to show him where to drill. He also told him to install an electric pump instead of a windmill.

After leaving the driller they stopped by the electric coop office and Ben explained to the service manager what he needed them to do. The manager told him they would get right on the job and get temporary power for the builders. By that time it was back to the cafe for lunch. Amos told Ben that he was going to make him gain so much weight that he couldn't get his britches on.

Ben told him that the Salvation Army store had bigger britches and that they would probably give him a couple of pair because he looked so down cast. Amos told him, "I guess they gave you a dozen pair the way you look."

"Old friend I got to admit every time I try to put something over on you, you back me in a corner like a pro boxer and lay me out cold. But I love every minute of it."

Amos replied, "Ben, you are the most enjoyable company I could ask for. I believe as you do, without humor life wouldn't be worth living."

"Amen Amos."

Ben dropped Amos at the parsonage and drove to Pepe's place. He asked where Joaquin was and Eva told him that he and Pepe left early this morning to rotate the Angora goats from one pasture to another but they should be back soon. The two cowboys went with them so they could finish before dark. Ben told Eva to have Joaquin call him when he got home. She said she would and Ben went home.

About an hour before dark Pepe called and said they had moved all of the goats and for him, Ruth and Maude to come and have supper with them in the bunk house with the cowboys. No one except Ben and Joaquin knew what Ben wanted to talk to him about. Eva tried to grill him but Joaquin only answered, "Who knows."

The meal was on the long table when they arrived. After supper was over Ben asked Joaquin to take a walk with him. All in the bunk house were held in suspense. Eva said, "I hope the boy is not in trouble and Ben fires him from his job."

Maude told Eva, "If he fires him I'll turn Amos loose on Ben."

They all looked from the bunkhouse windows trying to see what was going on. Ben would raise his arm and point and Joaquin would shake his head and point in another direction. They would walk a little farther and Ben made a few marks in the ground with his boot. Then a little ways farther he made some more scratches in the ground. Joaquin pointed to the east and Ben nodded his head. Eva shook her head and said, "I saw Ben shake his head when my son pointed to the east. I guess Ben was telling him to hit the road.

Ben called to Pepe and Eva, "We sure did enjoy the supper folks, we best be headed home. I guess you ladies have finished the dishes."

"We have been talking and don't worry about the dishes. I'm teaching our two cowboys about housekeeping."

Ben told Ruth and Maude to load up before Eva tries to get me to learn how to do house work too. After they had left Eva started questioning her son, "Did Ben fire you? What was going on out there? Are you in some kind of trouble? Why don't you answer me?"

Joaquin replied, "Mother, just wait and see, in due time you will understand everything."

Eva looked at Pepe as he sat quietly with a smile that told her she was defeated. She stomped her foot and left for the house as the four men had a good laugh at her expense.

After Eva had gone inside Joaquin told his dad he had to go to town and would be late getting back. He had a couple of things to do in the morning. Pepe said that he could handle things by himself, but if he needed any help let him know.

Pepe joined Eva and she asked, "Where is Joaquin going tonight? It isn't Saturday. I bet he is going to Ben and apologize for whatever he has done."

"Mama, he is not a little boy anymore. Why don't you quit worrying about him?"

Joaquin left Maria's home happy as a lark. He asked her dad for his daughters hand in marriage and he gave his blessing and said yes. Maria did also. He slept in the bunkhouse with the cowboys. He knew if he went to his bedroom Eva would not let him rest at all.

The next morning he located the spot for the new well and the driller and his helper went to work. As they were setting up the rig, the crew from the lumber company arrived with two trucks loaded with material. Joaquin showed them where the house was to be built and for the front door to face east. He missed breakfast because he didn't want to face Eva just yet.

At supper that night, in the bunkhouse, he explained everything to his parents with the two cowpokes listening and smiling. Tears flowed freely down Eva's' cheeks. Joaquin hoped they were tears of joy. They were.

A month later all was ready for the bride and groom. All that was left was to tie the knot. That created a problem. Eva said a priest should perform the ceremony. The couple would have Amos do it. Pepe told Eva she wasn't getting married and Amos was just as qualified as anyone. He said that Amos was closer to God than anyone else they knew. Amos would do it, period. The next Saturday the bride and groom, dressed in their Sunday best, stood in front of Minister Amos Brown on the front porch of the old Adams ranch house. Present were the Adams family, Pepe, Eva and Pepe's crew of cowboys, the two men in charge of the brush control and Slim Simmons and his wife Betty. Slim was the man Ben contracted to take care of all the farming for the ranch. He had worked several years for Ben. Marias' parents were also present.

Amos preformed the ceremony from memory. Heads were bowed, he said a short prayer, and then told them you are forever man and wife.

The ladies had prepared a luncheon of snacks with punch and lemonade for drinks. While they ate and talked a white pickup pulled up in the front drive and the owner of the lumber company called and ask for help. Ben and Pepe walked out to the truck as the man was moving a large cardboard box to the tailgate of the truck. Ben asked, "What did Maude order now?"

The man asked who Maude might be. Then he told Ben and Pepe that this was a gift from him and his employees for the newly married couple. The three of them carried it to the porch and called everyone to come and see the gift. The box was carefully opened and they all looked at the latest model of a Maytag washing machine with an electric motor and a swivel wringer. The owner told the crowd that this was the least he and his people could do to repay the business given to them by the folks at the Adams' ranch.

Ben said, "Bill Higgenbottom, you could not have given a better or more useful gift to this young couple. This just goes to show that the best people in the world live in West Texas. We all wish to thank you, not just for the gift you gave today, but what you give every day in goods, services and friendship to all the folks in our community."

At the end of Ben's little speech, Bill got a rousing

applause from the crowd.

Ben, Maude and Ruth gave the now married couple five hundred dollars to help furnish their new home. Slim and Betty gave a set of silverware while the cowboys had given a full set of nice dishware. Pepe and Eva were going to help with any more furnishings they would need. Amos presented them with a leather bound Bible. In gold letters on the front was engraved, Joaquin and Maria Rojas. Maria's parents gave the couple a new 1939 Ford coupe.

The newly married couple thanked everyone and then departed on a Saturday night honeymoon at the hotel in San Angelo. They knew if they didn't get away from the cowboys there would be no rest or peace this night. The two cow hands still believed in the old ways of really giving a newly married couple a rousing on their wedding night.

Ben, Amos, Ruth and Maude drove to town late that afternoon and had supper at the Western Steak House. After eating they dropped Amos off at the parsonage, bidding him good night, and they would see him in the morning.

Chapter Eight

Ruth began showing signs of motherhood as the days went from weeks to months and the time for the fall roundup began. The bunkhouse was full of cowboys that were ripping, raring and ready.

The old ways were gone. Horses were hauled to the pastures in large goose neck trailers, already saddled. The days of the horse wrangler was a job of the past, as was the camp cook and the chuck wagon. Ice chest were packed with cold drinks and sack lunches. Coffee that would float a horse shoe went with the chuck wagon. The branding irons were heated with a butane burner instead of a good mesquite fire.

There were a few things that always were the same, dust, the smell of scorched hair from the hot iron, manure on your boots and elsewhere, and above all the typical cowboy; the jingle of his spurs, his hat, bandana, and his language. To the old timers like Ben and Pepe these things brought good old memories.

After the spring calves were marked, branded and doctored for screw worms, they were turned back to their mothers. Then the process was repeated in the next pasture. Ben or Pepe picked out the older cows to be shipped to market with the two year old steers.

The Adams ranch consisted of sixty-two sections of land or sixty-two square miles or thirty-nine-thousand-six hundred and eighty acres. The location was a rectangle being six miles wide and ten miles long with two sections adjoining the rectangle on the North West corner. All the sections were fenced and cross fenced with four gates at the intersecting corners. This made it easy to rotate the cattle from one pasture to another. It took a week to finish the roundup and get the cattle that were ready for market in the holding pens, keeping the steers separated from the older cows. Ben ran about six hundred head of mother cows and always kept enough heifers to replace the older cows he sold each year. The new diesel trucks were backed up to the loading gates and the work began again. These older cows were easier to load than the steers so they were loaded and hauled to the sale barn first. The total tally to be sold was four hundred and sixty two, which Ben figured it would be about twenty trips for each truck. They hauled the last four loads after dark, and after the last steers were unloaded Ben took Pepe, Joaquin and the two cowboys to the steak house for supper. Ben thanked them for a job well done and tomorrow would be a catch up day. When Joaquin asked what a catch up day was, Ben told him to catch up on your sleep.

September ended with all of the crops harvested and in the barn. The oats and wheat planted to be cut next spring for winter hay. It had been a very good year for the Adams ranch. The best was yet to come.

Thanksgiving was again a time of fellowship with the four Rojas family present and the two cowboys. Amos gladly offered thanks for the bountiful meal prepared by the four ladies. Ruth was heavy with child, and she reminded Ben of how Elsie looked just before James was born. Ben missed his wife more than anything else. He would give all he owned to have her now. But life goes on.

Ruth received mail almost daily from James and kept them informed as to how things were with him. He had been transferred to Wright-Patterson Air Force Base and the training was intense. The army had put up temporary quarters with six men to each little building. It was so cold that water would freeze inside at night. He wished he could be home for the holiday, but no one was allowed off base until training was completed. He hoped he could be home before the baby was due. The military was not likely to let anyone have furlough until this phase of training was complete.

Amos stayed with them until Ben took him home on Saturday. They had breakfast together and Amos told Ben to keep a sharp eye on Ruth as she was due at any time. Ben told him he and Maude was with her all the time and would call him when they started for the hospital.

The evening of December sixth Maude told Ben to get the car warmed up that it was time to be prepared to leave for the hospital at anytime. Ben gave Amos a call and then brought the car around front and left the motor running with the heater on. He started up the porch steps as Maude and Ruth were coming out. Ben opened the rear door and helped Ruth in. She gave Ben a smile and told him that this time tomorrow he would be a grandfather. With Maude in the back with Ruth, Ben took off for town like a shot out of a cannon. Maude told him to slow down or she would drive. He slowed down in a hurry. Amos was in the waiting room when they arrived. The two nurses took Ruth into the delivery room which was next to the waiting area.

The Seth Thomas clock on the wall was at nine p.m. Amos sat relaxed in an overstuffed chair while Maude sat looking thru a stack of magazines. Ben walked the floor and drank coffee and went to the rest room. After four trips to the coffee pot and the restroom, Amos told Ben, "You are not having this baby, why don't you sit down and relax. There is not one thing you can do except wear out the floor and the toilet. At the rate you are going now we will to have you admitted in here before the baby arrives."

Ben said, "Amos, I'm glad you came along so you can look out for my welfare. Maude doesn't like my driving and you don't like my walking. I think I'll just have myself admitted so I want be such a bother to you perfect people."

Maude spoke, "I think that is the best idea he's had yet, don't you Amos?"

"With you two ganging up on me I don't stand a chance."

The hours passed so slowly that Ben thought the clock might be running backwards. He had emptied the coffee pot twice and made a dozen trips to the restroom.

He was thinking this may be a false alarm when all of a sudden a cry that rattled the windows came from the delivery room. Amos came alive and so did Maude. Ben said, "If that was the baby he sure has got a strong set of lungs. If he can eat like he can bawl he will be a big boy before you know it."

After a few minutes the doctor came out and said, "Mr. Adams, you have an eight-pound-eight-ounce very healthy grandson. As soon as the nurses get things cleaned up they will take Ruth to the room across the hall. You all may visit her and the baby for a few minutes if you like." Ben thanked the doctor and sat for the first time in the last ten hours.

James Benjamin Adams was born on December seventh, nineteen-hundred and forty, in the Texas Mercy Hospital, San Angelo Texas to the proud parents, James and Ruth Adams. The boy will be better known as Little Ben.

Three days later Little Ben got his first ride in a horseless carriage. Ben was driving so slow Maude asked if he was asleep. "If I drive fast you gripe, if I drive slow you gripe, I'm just taking it easy so Little Ben can see the sights."

"Well the cars behind you don't care about the sightseeing tour. They have better things to do than just poke along."

Ben pulled to the side to let the others pass. They didn't. The man behind them got out of his car and walked up to Ben who was rolling down his window. It was Slim Simmons.

Slim said, "Ease on up to the ranch Ben. We all are following so we can get a good look at Little Ben. You are driving a little fast to be caring such a precious cargo."

"Slim, my back seat driver thinks I'm going to slow, but I'll see if I can slow down a notch or two. All you folks just come on and we will have some refreshments. I won't charge you anything to look at my grandson."

Slim said, "Go ahead on, we will be right behind you."

Ben did. Maude kept quiet, Ruth laughed.

Four carloads of people from the church viewed the baby while Maude and Betty prepared some snacks and put on a large pot of coffee. Ben had a good idea who was behind this visitation. Amos was playing the part of the godfather as he never left his place beside Ruth while the visitors got a good look at Little Ben. Amos was as happy as if the baby was his own. Ben thought to himself, when God created Amos He sure knew what He was doing.

As the crowd was beginning to depart, Ben asked Amos if he would spend the afternoon with them. He told him that he would take him home after supper. Amos said he would be delighted to. Ben figured that Amos would like to spend as much time playing with the baby as he could. After losing his wife Ben knew how lonesome Amos must be living by himself.

Ruth got a call from James telling her that he has a thirty day furlough and would fly to Lackland on an Army cargo plane and arrive on the twentieth. He asked if they would pick him up around six in the afternoon. Yes they would.

Ben got his first look at the huge base; aircraft were taking off and landing. Planes were parked in perfect rows on the tarmac. As they watched, a twin engine plane landed and taxied to the area where they were parked. After the propellers quit turning the rear door opened as a ground crew placed a set of steps up to the door. James was the first one off and hurried to meet them. He hugged and kissed Ruth and got his first look at his son. It was a happy time for the

Adams family.

Ben stopped in the little town of Kerrville where they had supper. James had matured and was a handsome figure with his uniform on. Ben could see the strain the training was having upon him and from being away from his wife and son.

He hoped that this war would be like a West Texas dust storm and just blow itself out. They arrived home late, but sleep would have to wait as the family sat by the fireplace and visited. Little Ben had been in the land of nod since dark, and was still held in James's arms.

Ben was up before daylight and quietly slipped out. He knew that if he didn't get to town and pick Amos up that he would call and wake everyone up. They all sat up late and Ben knew how tired they were. He knew Amos would want to see James as soon as he could. Ben banged on the door and called for Amos to open up. Amos said, "You could have been here earlier, I figured you would show up around four o'clock."

"If I knew you would of been up I would have made it at three o'clock. I figured you needed your beauty sleep. However you could sleep a month and it wouldn't help your looks a bit. If you will get yourself dressed I'll buy breakfast."

Amos was in such a hurry he had to tie his shoes while Ben drove to the restaurant. They sat in the pickup for about ten minutes before they opened up. Amos told Ben that he got him up to early. Ben told Amos that he could haul him back if he needed to sleep that bad. Amos told Ben he didn't want him to because he would try to make him pay a fare like his old pickup was a taxi cab. While they ate Ben told Amos why he got him out of bed so early. Amos told Ben he understood. They sat and talked for an hour and then headed for the ranch. These two men were closer than brothers.

James hugged Amos like he was his grandfather

instead of the local minister. Amos was hugging too.

Amos and Ben had coffee while the others ate breakfast. James said if he had known that his dad was going to get Amos he would have joined them. Amos told James that he needed to spend every second with his wife and son, and he wanted a picture of the three of them before James had to return to duty.

Chapter Nine

As Christmas was approaching, the ladies started planning; Eva said the best place to have the large dinner was the bunkhouse. They agreed and started a list of preparations. What to cook, how much, what to drink, how much, how many and what kind of pies, what about decorations, the list went on and on.

Ben's twin girls, Marlene and Arlene, called and told him that they would be coming home for the holidays and would stay until after New Years. Ben didn't get to see much of the girls as they lived in a world of their own. They would call once in a while but hardly ever would he receive a letter from them. Ben and Elsie had set up a bank account for them when they started to college and they proved to be very self sufficient. As hard as Ben tried, he never could seem to make the two understand his love for them.

The long holidays were a joy to all. Plenty of good eats, remembering old times and old friends, but all things must end. The twins left to return to college and James to Lackland to catch another military plane to Wright-Patterson. It was a lonely trip back to the ranch after they told James goodbye. Ruth held back her tears as did Maude. Ben could only hope that his son would return safely home when this war was over. He knew Amos said a special prayer for James each night as millions of others would do for their loved ones before this world wide conflict would end.

Winter turned to spring and spring to summer and Little Ben was growing like a weed. The twins came for a visit one week end and brought with them two young men they introduced as their friends, Steve Johns and Carl Benson. They were classmates from New York and had never visited a Texas ranch, so the girls agreed to show them the ranch where they had grown up.

The tour of the ranch fell upon Ben to give these big city boys a look see of a real working ranch. After an all day trip they could not comprehend all that large amount of land, the horses, the cattle, sheep and goats. They watched real cowboys on real horses doing real work. They watched as Slim Simmons directed his crew cutting, raking and baling hay. The barns, sheds, the bunkhouse, the ranch houses, it was a self contained little world. They could not believe that one man could own and operate such a place as this.

This man, Ben Adams, wasn't all dressed up like a Wall Street business man or a New York banker. He didn't talk like one either. You couldn't tell him from one of the people working for him. A devious thought entered devious minds as people with lust for things that they desire belong to others.

After the twins dropped the guys off at their dorm Carl asked Steve, "How would you like to own half of that Adams ranch? I've been doing a lot of thinking of how easy it could be."

"Why don't you clue me in, if you are thinking what I am, all we have to do is marry the twins. I don't want to have to live in a faraway place like where it's located. We would be miles from any entertainment and the life style that we both love. Besides that old man might out live both of us."

"I'm not planning to live there very long. All we have to do is get Adams committed to an old folks home claiming he's not mentally competent. We could con the girls into helping without them knowing it. Once we got him in a mental institution then we could marry the girls. Then talk them into selling the place and we could live like kings the rest of our lives."

Steve asked, "Just how do you plan to get a doctor to prove that Adams has got to many loose screws to be able to think for himself? You can't just ask someone to commit him without proof. That old man could out think both of us in a deal like this."

Carl replied, "A little payola in the hand of a pro can do anything. I know a guy in New York that for a few hundred bucks could get a doctor down here that could get the president committed.

"We need to gradually start working on the twins to where they tell Adams that he really needs to go into a good clinic, and get a complete physical. While he is in the clinic our doctor could give him a load of some mind altering drugs that for a few days he wouldn't know who he is or where he's from. Once they put him in the nut house we could marry the girls and after a while talk them into selling the ranch. There is no telling what that place with all of the stock and equipment is worth. Think about it, this time next year we could be millionaires." They both agreed to put the plan in action.

As time went by they dropped little hints to the twins about their dad feeling dizzy while they drove thru the ranch or that he couldn't remember little things like where they were from. As the days went by they began to suggest that Ben should have a complete examination both physical and mental. Carl said that his father had a good friend who was an expert physiologist and that he could get him to fly down. He and Steve would pay for his trip and service. They explained that they were concerned about their dad's health. The girls promised to get Ben into a clinic as soon as they could. Carl told the twins it would be better if their dad didn't know that they were trying to help. It might give him the wrong impression that they were trying to tend to something that didn't concern them, and the last thing they wanted was for Ben to have hard feelings toward them. The twins said they understood and were grateful for their concern.

Back at the ranch Ben was preparing for the fall

hunting season in Colorado, with his two boyhood friends, Buddy Rose, the banker, and Earl Biggs, the lawyer who was elected district judge. They had missed last season because the judge had a trial on the docket he had to preside over. Ben furnished the truck, trailer, horses and all of the camping gear. The season started the middle of October and lasted two weeks.

It was a good time to get away and enjoy a good hunt with friends you made before you were in the first grade. Ben had all of the gear in the storage bin in the front of the trailer as well as three saddles and tack for the three horses they would ride and the three pack horses. He had the six horses in a corral with the trailer backed to the loading gate. His rifle and other personal gear were locked in the tool box on the truck bed. It would still be a few days before they left. He wanted to have the horses in top shape and not have to hurry at the last minute.

Ben had received a letter from the twins saying they were concerned about his health and wanted him to take a complete physical. They had made him an appointment at the Mayo Clinic and Rest home. They called him a couple of times and wanted to make sure he was in good shape before he left to go hunting. Ben felt that if the twins thought that much of him that he should do it. It would be an overnight stay but it was a few days before he left for Colorado. The twins showed up early the morning of his trip to the doctor and Carl and Steve was with them. Maude made sure he had bathed and shaved. Ben kissed Little Ben goodbye and rode to the clinic with the girls and their friends.

Ben was checked over by the clinics medical doctor very carefully and the doctor told Ben to walk around their facility and to make himself at home. He wanted him to come back by his office in an hour or so. He told him he wanted to check his blood pressure again.

The twins and their friends had gone out for a late lunch, so Ben wandered up the stairs to the second floor. Going down the hall he looked into the bed rooms noting that there were two beds to each room. Every room he looked at had both beds occupied except the last room on the right. As he paused at the door, the man in the bed looked very familiar. He took a step inside and spoke to the elderly man. "Epp Hardin, is that you laying in that bed this time of day?"

The old cowboy uttered, "Well, I swun if it ain't Ben Adams. Son, I haven't seen you in a coon's age. You are a site for sore eyes. If I could jump out of this bed I'd hug your neck. The last time I saw you was when you came up to Sterling City. You helped me roundup that bunch of steers that got out of my pasture into my neighbors place after that drunk driver tore down fences for a half a mile up and down the highway. I always thought you was as good a cowboy as I ever laid eyes on. What in tarnation are you doing in a place like this?"

Ben explained to Epp the reason he was here and that he had to spend the night to see another doctor from New York in the morning.

Epp replied, "Don't do it Ben. That's what got me in this stinking place. It happened to me just like it's fixing to happen to you. My kids thought I wasn't able to take care of myself. They pulled the same stunt on me that they are fixing to put over on you. When they put you to bed tonight they will give you a pill that will make you so absent minded you won't know who you are or where you are from. You are in the prime of life Ben, for heaven's sake don't let them do this to you.

"Stick that pill under your tongue and spit it out after the nurse leaves. This room is the only one that has a vacant bed so I'm sure that they will put you in here with me. Just prepare yourself to sneak out of here about midnight. I'll show you how easy it can be done.

"Have someone you can trust to meet you over on the south side of the building. You will need for them to bring you a complete change of clothes, boots and all because they will take all your clothes and wallet. They will give you a pair of these rags like I have on to wear. If you don't want to wind up like me Ben, you better take my advice; you are too good of a person for this to happen to."

Ben told Epp that he would be back up as soon as the doctor finished up with his physical exam. Back downstairs Ben needed to visit the toilet before seeing the doctor. There were four stalls in the toilet. Being modest, Ben took the last stall away from the lavatories. After seating himself he heard someone else enter. It was Carl and Steve back from lunch. Not knowing Ben was there, Steve asked, "Do you think the twins have any idea of what we are up to?"

"Not unless you slipped up and said something you shouldn't have. I believe they think we are doing this because we care about the old man. If they even dreamed we were after the ranch they would shoot us. As soon as our fake New York doctor gets him committed we are on easy street."

After they washed up and left, Ben felt a great relief that his children were not a part of the plot. He also knew that Epp was right about everything he had told him. The first thought he had was to beat the living daylights out of the two guys who had put the twins up to this big steal. No, why not let these two and the quack doctor spend some time down at Huntsville in the state pen.

Ben left the toilet and walked to the pay phone booth in the lobby and called Pepe. Ben spoke in Spanish and told Pepe to do the same. Ben told him what to bring and where to meet him and at what time but not to tell anyone about what was going on, not even Eva or Amos. Pepe understood that something serious was happening and Ben would explain it when he wanted to.

Ben then went to finish up with the local doctor. After the test was completed Ben asked the doctor if he could introduce him to the doctor from New York. In an office down the hall Ben was introduced to Dr. Samuel Viszo. As Ben started to leave he asked very politely if he might have the doctor's business card. The small beady eyed man was happy to hand Ben a fancy engraved card with the doctors name address and phone number. Ben thanked him and said he would see him in the morning.

He returned to the lobby and, with smiles, told the twins and the boys that the doctor gave him a clean bill of health. He told them to go on home as he had to spend the night and see the last doctor in the morning. He asked them to pick him up around noon. The twins gave him a hug and told him to get a good night's sleep.

A nurse took him upstairs to the room where Epp was and left him pajamas. She told him to change and she would be back soon with their supper. When the nurse closed the door Epp told Ben to hide his wallet and other personal stuff under the mattress of his bed or they would take it too. Ben did. When the nurse brought their food she got Ben's clothes, and asked if he had any valuables she could put in the safe for him. He told her no, and asked what she was going to do with his clothes. She said they would be in a locker in the store room and he could get them when he was dismissed.

About nine o'clock another nurse came to pick up the supper trays and handed Ben a small paper cup with a yellow colored pill in it and told him to take it as she handed him a glass of water. Ben stuck the pill under his tongue and swallowed the water. As soon as the nurse left Ben spit the pill out and flushed it down the toilet. At ten o'clock there was a bed check and the door to their room was locked. Epp told Ben that at two there would be another bed check and he needed to wait an hour or so before he made his escape, by then everyone would be asleep.

The hour passed and Ben removed the screen from the casement window as Epp directed, then rolled his bed against the wall by the window. Then he twisted the sheets, tied them together and tied one end to the bed post. He pitched the other end out the window and walked over to Epp. Ben told Epp, "If you want to go with me I'll lower you down first."

"Ben, I'm nearly ninety years old and I can't hardly walk or get out of this bed by myself. I would give up my best roping horse if I could. All I ask that you drop by to visit me when you get this mess over with."

Ben shook the feeble hand and promised Epp he would be back. Then as he started crawling out of the window Epp warned him of the rose bushes at the end of the sheets.

Ben found the bushes, thorns and all. Pepe was at the meeting place and Ben discarded his pajamas and changed into the clothes Pepe had brought him. He told Pepe to stop at the first phone booth. Ben called Earl and apologized for calling so late but it was something he would explain later. He told Earl and Buddy to meet him in Pagosa Springs on Friday around noon at Jan's Cafe.

Ben told him not to let anyone know where he was. Just bring their personal gear that he had all the rest. Pepe let Ben out at the shed by the horse corral and Ben told him to take care of everything. Just play dumb as to what was going on and let no one know where he was. Ben then loaded the horses up and slipped into his bedroom and got his duffle bag with his small personal things. He then started on the eight hundred mile trip to the high country.

Chapter Ten

Buddy and Earl had arrived late Thursday night, and Ben noticed Buddy's Buick across the street at a log cabin motel. Ben and Elsie had spent a few days there on vacation years ago. Ben looked in the cafe window and glanced at his two old friends waiting. As he joined them, he knew he had a lot of explaining to do, but not here. After a good meal they got checked out of the motel and Buddy left his car at the Chevrolet dealers to be serviced. He would pick it up when they started home.

Leaving town Ben drove to the edge of the national forest where he had parked the trailer. He had three saddle horses and a pack horse in the trailer. Ben jumped the horses out as Earl and Buddy unloaded their gear and packed their personal things on the pack horse. All three men had spent a good part of their lives in a saddle and hunted several seasons in this area. It was kind of like a second home.

It was sunset when they reached the camp which Ben had set up on the back side of Flat Top Mountain. Very few hunters knew of the trail that crossed the Coffee Cup Ranch before you could enter the National Forest to get to this area. Ben told his friends that they would probably be the only ones in this area. Buddy got a fire going as Ben helped Earl unpack and unroll their sleeping bags in the tent. Buddy cooked supper while Earl and Ben hobbled the horses and left them with the others. After the meal, Buddy asked Ben, "Well old friend, are you ready to tell us about your quick disappearance?"

Ben went into detail about his experience at the hospital. When he finished he took the card the he had placed in his wallet before they had taken his clothes and handed it to Earl.

Ben asks of Earl, "Is there any way I could get these

three shysters installed in the state pen?"

Earl studied the card and replied, "I think I've read an article about this quack before. If I'm not mistaken he had a lawsuit filed on him for trying the same kind of a deal in Utah. I can't remember what the verdict was, but it sure raised a stink. Let me keep this card and I'll sure look into the matter. For the next two weeks let us just leave our worries behind and enjoy ourselves." They did.

At the end of the second week they were packed and headed for town and a hot bath and shave. The hunt was successful as most of their hunts were, but it was just being outdoors and enjoying their long friendship that made the hunt really count.

The next morning Earl asked Buddy, "Would you mind riding home with Ben, I need to have the use of your car for a couple of days. Since we are this close to Moab, Utah I want to drive over there and talk to a few people about that lawsuit. I'll see if I might pick up some information in person that I might not get otherwise."

Buddy told Earl he could take the car and hoped he could find enough information to help Ben put these people away for a long time. Earl headed west while Buddy and Ben went south. Pulling the large trailer, loaded with all their gear, the horses and the game they had killed, was a hard pull until they entered central New Mexico and left the mountains behind.

Eighteen hours later they were unloading the horses and gear at Ben's corrals. Ben told Buddy to take his pickup and use it until Earl returned his car. Buddy left for home and Ben finished unloading his gear. He put the dressed game they had killed in his ice house and after a shower he crawled into bed. It had been a long day. At breakfast Ben explained to Ruth and Maude the reason for his disappearance and why he didn't want anyone to know of his whereabouts. Maude told him that the twins were worried about him and the two boys with them acted scared. They asked the twins to get the law to try to find you. The girls told them that you could take care of yourself and you had a good reason to leave the clinic or you would have stayed. Ben said that he would call the twins and let them know the reason. He did not want them to say anything to the boys that would alarm them into warning the quack, or them trying to cut and run. Ruth heard Little Ben wanting to be fed so after Ruth had nursed him; Ben took control of his grandson.

After he was sure Pepe had all of the hands doing their jobs for the day he drove to his home and explained to he and Eva the reason he left so mysteriously. Eva said, "I can't believe anyone could be that evil. I hope Judge Biggs can get all three put in jail for a long time. If he can't you and Pepe should take a bull whip to their rear ends."

Pepe told Ben that everything at the ranch was going good; all of the hay was stored in the barns and the grain was in the silos. They were ready for winter. Slim Simmons had serviced all of the farm equipment and it was all put away for next season. Ben told Pepe he had to go to town and asked if he needed to pick anything up for him. Pepe said, "If you can find some pills that would keep Eva from being so grouchy to me it would be nice."

"You old man, I should take a whip to you. You just don't know how good of a wife I am to you."

Ben smiled and said, "I'd better get some pills for both of you."

Ben picked up the frozen meat that belonged to Buddy and told the ladies that he was going to town and if they want to go shopping while he ran a few errands to come along. They did. Ben dropped them off downtown and stopped at the bank to tell Buddy about his meat. Buddy left word with a cashier that he would be out for a while. Ben drove to

Buddy's place and they stored the meat in his freezer. Ben took Buddy back to the bank and his next stop was at the clinic. He wanted to fulfill his promise to Epp. Epp was glad to see him and told him that he had given the doctors a bad scare. Epp said they gave him the third degree trying to find out where you were and why you escaped.

"I told them I didn't know and didn't care, but if I was able I'd have gone with you. Wherever you were had to be better than this nut house."

Ben explained to Epp the whole story and wished that Epp could have made the trip to the mountains. They talked for a while and Ben told him he would visit him the next trip to town.

Ben claimed the clothes they had taken. The resident doctor asked him to see him in his office. The doctor asked why he left without seeing the New York doctor. He said that Dr. Viszo was quite upset and left the clinic saying that you needed to be committed to our facility as soon as possible.

Ben asked, "Doctor, do you think that I've got a loose screw? Would you like to be confined to this place like Epp Hardin just because your children didn't want you around? My mind and health is better than most men my age. You ran a complete physical on me, and what did you find wrong?"

"Mr. Adams, when I get your age I can only hope that I will be as healthy and in as good of physical condition as you. It is not for me to say what Dr. Viszo may have said about your mental condition. I believe that your brain is in better shape than most people that come to this clinic. I wouldn't want you to think that I or my staff had anything to do with requesting Dr. Viszo to examine you. I have in my files a letter from him asking the date of your visit, saying he was requested to exam you personally. Who ever asked him to do so I do not know?"

"May I have that letter doctor?" Ben asked.

"Sir, I can't do that as it is our policies that all correspondence is kept in our files. Only a court order can retrieve it. I can assure you that the order would have to come from a District judge like Judge Earl Biggs who happens to be a patient of mine and also a good friend. And I know he and Buddy Rose are as close as brothers." Ben gave the doctor a smile, thanked him and after a firm handshake left.

The letter Viszo addressed to the clinic stated that some of Ben's family in Dallas had requested Viszo to exam Ben. Ben knew the doctor had a conversation in confidence with Epp because Epp had told him about the people in Dallas.

Two days later Judge Biggs called and asked Ben to join him and a couple of friends for lunch in the private dining room at the downtown hotel. When Ben entered he was surprised to see the clinic doctor present.

The other gentleman was introduced as Marvin McCloud, a retired F.B.I. officer. After the meal Earl handed him an opened letter, it was from Dr. Viszo stating that some of Mister Ben Adam's kin asked if he would exam a Mr. Ben Adams of San Angelo, Texas at the Mayo Clinic. That as Ben would be present there soon; he should contact the clinic for the date of Mr. Adams appointment. Would they please call so he could make sure that airline reservations could be made in time to correspond with Mr. Adams visit.

Ben replied, "I have no family in Dallas or anywhere else. My twin daughters are in college in Waco and my son is in the military."

"Will you please tell me about the two boys that visited your ranch with your girls the first time you met them," McCloud asked.

"They were introduced to me as Steve Johns and Carl Benson. My girls told me they were from New York and had never seen a working ranch, so they invited them to spend a weekend with us at the ranch. I drove them in an all day tour around the place and explained the general working of what ranch life was. They asked a few questions about different things but showed no real interest. Both were just a couple of boys that the girls knew, and I really didn't take much interest in them after we got back to the house."

Ben told them of the conversation he overheard in the restroom at the clinic and his visit with Epp Hardin and decided that he best disappear for awhile. He wanted to talk with Earl about what best to do with these three con artists.

McCloud told them that this Viszo character had several complaints like this but no one had enough proof to get him in court. "I have an idea of how we might get him this time, but we may have to let one of the boys off easy if he will turn state's evidence. With the Judge's permission I would love to proceed with my plan."

"Permission granted, by all means you have all of my support and thanks, and I think we all agree to move as quickly as possible." replied Judge Biggs.

"Mr. McCloud, you could find out from my twins which of the two boys would be the weakest. I've told them of the plot, and not to let the boys have any idea that anyone knows what they had planned."

As they left the meeting Ben walked to the doctor's car with him and told him how much he appreciated the stand he had taken. "Ben, after I had spoken to Epp I knew I had to do something, so I called the judge to explain what had taken place. He was the one who told me about the court order for the letter. I felt very bad about this and hope it doesn't give the clinic a bad image."

Ben told him it would help not only the clinic, but its staff and patients. It would show the community you are doing the right thing to keep this from happening to someone else. Ben drove by the church and found Amos in the church study preparing his sermon for the coming Sunday.

"Well, I see that the runaway son has returned to ask for my forgiveness. I knew that you had a problem that you didn't want to worry me with so I thought I'd pray for you since you don't know how to pray for yourself. I hope God has answered my prayers."

Ben told Amos the whole story explaining that neither Maude nor Ruth knew where he was or why he left without telling them. "I just wanted to think things out and see what Earl thought was the best course to take. I believe we have everything headed in the right direction after this meeting today. I hope that the judge will make this bunch sorry they ever tried such a stunt as this."

"Ben, it is an awful thing when people would sink so low that they would try to steal a man's home, using his children as tools of the devil to do so, and then trying to have you committed to an asylum for the rest of your life. I also hope the judge teaches them a lesson they will never forget."

"Amos, I need to ask a favor of you. Epp Hardin is an old cowboy that is going to die on the second floor of that clinic. I am the only visitor he has had. I would appreciate it if you would pay him a visit when you get a chance and let him know that I thank him so much for helping me. If it had not been for him I would be laying right beside him."

"Ben, I'll go this afternoon and pay him a visit and give him your thanks."

Ben left Amos and headed back to the ranch to continue spoiling his grandson. The boy was one of the greatest treasures Ben could ever hope for. Little Ben was James made over. Ruth, Maude and Eva thought the sun rose and set in him. Ben wished that James could be with him in these precious times. Maybe James would get a long furlough for Christmas like last year.

The middle of November Earl called Ben to tell him

that McCloud had a confession from Steve Johns, and that he had gotten an arrest warrant for Carl Benson and Samuel Viszo. All three were in the Tom Green county jail with bail set so high that they could not make bond and were bound over for trial.

Viszo's lawyer would represent all three and had asked for a change of venue, which was denied as was a request for a postponement. The trial date was set for the Monday after the Thanksgiving Holidays were over. Texas justice was swift and sure. Lawbreakers beware. At nine a.m. the bailiff called the court in session and had all to rise as Earl entered. The judge went through the opening formalities quickly and got down to business in an expedient manner. Witnesses were called, sworn in, and the defense attorney started his objections and the judge started his overruling.

At one point the defense lawyer said that Dr. Viszo was the wrong man to be on trial.

Earl replied, "Viszo is not his real name, he changed it after spending five years in the pen in New Jersey for trying a stunt like this in that state. Your client has a rap sheet so long it took a half of a day to read it. I can't see where we are trying the wrong man."

Summations were made and the case was handed to the jury. Ben left for the restroom and when he returned the jury was reseated and Earl asked if they had reached a verdict. Yes they had. All three were guilty as charged. Earl sentenced Viszo and Benson to twenty years in the state pen, and because of his help and turning state's witness Steve Johns was put on parole for one year.

Amos told Ben that Texas justice was almost as fast as what the Good Lord could dish out but not quite as severe.

After the trial Ben thanked all of the ones who put an end to these people who preyed on others.

Chapter Eleven

December the first arrived and with it came James. Home for the holidays, but more importantly his son's first birthday. Ruth was overjoyed at seeing her husband wearing his uniform with the silver bars of a first lieutenant.

Ben and Maude were out of the picture until James finally turned loose of Ruth and with Little Ben on one arm gave his dad and aunt a hug with the other arm.

Questions were asked and answered; how was everyone and everything? Is Amos doing alright? What about Pepe and Eva? How are Joaquin and Maria? What was all of this about you disappearing for two weeks? Ben told James to slow down for a while; we don't have time to answer you before you ask another. We would like to know a little about you.

They all sat up late and enjoyed one another's company, just relaxing and talking. James would not turn loose of his son. He was so happy just to set and hold him. Ruth told James that Little Ben could walk if he would put him on the floor.

"I want to hold him forever, I have missed you and the baby so much, and I could hardly wait to get home. The worst part of military life is being away from your family. Thank goodness I only have four years and seven months left on my tour of duty."

The next morning Ben, James and Little Ben made a trip to visit with the Rojas families. Eva gave James a big hug and told him they were so happy to see him. Eva and Maria served coffee and doughnuts while they chatted. James talked with Pepe and Joaquin about the ranch while Ben fed doughnuts to his grandson. When they were ready to leave Eva handed Ben a sack of the doughnuts and said they were for Little Ben.

Ben called Amos and asked if he would like to go to

lunch with him.

Yes he would if he could pay for the meal. Ben told them all to get ready to surprise Amos. Ben honked the horn in front of the parsonage and out came his old friend. When Amos got to the car he stopped in his tracks. James just picked him up while giving him a bear hug. Tears were in Amos's eyes as he was so glad to see James. Amos got in the rear seat with Ruth, Maude and Little Ben. Ruth handed the little boy to Amos who held him until they arrived at the restaurant.

Finishing their coffee after the meal, Ruth told Amos that they were planning a birthday party for Little Ben after Sunday morning services and wanted Amos to come. The Rojas family would be present as well as Slim and Betty.

James said, "Amos, I will drag you out of the church as soon as the closing prayer is over. You don't need to preach a two hour sermon or visit with the two old maids that corner you at the close of every service. Amos, Just slip out the back door and we will grab a quick lunch and head for the ranch."

"A short sermon won't be a problem but you know I have to keep Gladys Henley and Matilda Maynard on the straight and narrow pathway."

Maude said, "Amos, those two women have been trying to get their hooks in you for so long I thought they would give up by now."

"Their hooks, as you call them, will not penetrate my suit of armor." Amos got free of the old maids and met James at the rear door of the church. They had a quick lunch and were ready for the birthday bash.

Somewhere around three o'clock Ruth told Ben there was a phone call for him. Ben talked on the phone for a couple of minutes and hung up.

When he returned to the party he asked for silence.

Everyone stopped and looked at Ben.

"Folks, I hate to tell you the news. Buddy Rose just called me and said that the Japs have bombed Pearl Harbor, killing many and destroying several ships and airplanes. I think we should turn on the radio and listen to the news."

A grim silence came over the party as report after report came over the airways. None of them were good. Wave after wave of Japanese torpedo planes and dive bombers as well as fighter aircraft brought death and destruction to the islands in the Pacific.

The President was calling an emergency meeting of the Congress. America was drawn into the conflict that the rest of the world was in whether Americans wanted it or not. Today was the beginning of a world crisis, and it was Little Ben's first birthday.

After they had all departed for the evening the Adams family sat in the living room, each with their own thoughts. Ruth asked, "James, what will this do to your furlough?"

"I think all military personnel will be ordered back to base immediately. The morning news will let us know as soon as the order is given. From what I understand, Germany has a pact with Japan. When Japan attacks America, Germany will declare war on America.

"However the news never mentioned that Japan declared war on America. I guess they wanted to destroy as much of our Pacific Fleet as possible with a sneak attack. America will declare war on Japan tomorrow then Hitler will probably declare war on us. That means America will be fighting on two fronts on opposite sides of the world. It is a strategy designed to drain our manpower and resources. On top of that we will have to help all of the Allied Forces around the world. As it is, we are poorly equipped to fight on one front let alone two. F.D.R. will start the wheels of the nation to rolling tomorrow. The bleeding hearts in Congress will be astride a war horse now instead of a Shetland pony.

They can change their speeches faster than a speeding bullet."

James was correct. The early morning news repeated the recall of all military personnel to report to their home bases immediately.

The five of the Adams family left for Lackland as soon as breakfast was finished. Ben drove with Maude in the front seat telling him how to drive. Ben ignored her, but that didn't slow her down. James, Ruth and Little Ben sat in the back seat with James holding him. James had told Ben to drive without stopping if possible. It would be hard to catch a hop as it was going to be so many trying to get to their bases. Of course they just had to make a pit stop or two along the way.

They arrived just before noon and James checked with the officer in charge. There was a flight departing for Wright-Patterson in half an hour and he could board anytime.

Ben got James's duffle bag from the trunk of his car and carried it to the flight gate where the four were telling James goodbye. Ben took Little Ben from James and motioned for Maude to step away. She did. It was a hard thing to watch as Ruth tearfully kissed her husband and told him goodbye.

They all stood at the gate and watched the plane taxi to the long runway and depart with their loved one. When they started home Ben suggested to Maude to set in the back with Ruth and help her overcome her emotions. She would. On the drive home Ben tried, but could not comprehend what was going to happen in the next few years. It was so senseless for someone to try to conquer and control the entire world. He wondered how many would die and how many maimed for life. How many wives and mothers would lose husbands and sons? Ben hoped Amos could give him an understanding of some kind.

Chapter Twelve

On the morning of Christmas Eve, Ben and Amos
visited Epp Hardin at the clinic. Epp was glad to see them but
he told them that he had not been feeling well the last couple
of days. They chatted with Epp for a while and Ben could tell
that Epp was a lot weaker than his visit with him last week.
They wished him a Merry Christmas and told him they would
see him next week.

Downstairs Ben asked Amos to come with him as he
wanted to see Doctor Vernon Horton for a few minutes.

The doctor asked them both to be seated and wanted to
know if he could be of help.

Ben asked, "Sir, have you seen Epp the last few days?
We just came from his room and he explained to us that he
had not felt to good the last couple of days. I noticed that he
was not himself as he usually is. He looked tired and weak.
I'm afraid that he might have the flu."

"Yes, I've checked on him every day for the past two
weeks. Epp's heart is just worn out. The heart is designed to
last just so long and his has lasted longer than most. As the
heart gets weaker it pumps less blood to the body and it
finally stops. This is what's happing to Epp."

"How much longer has he got?" Ben asked.

"A few weeks at the most, it's hard to tell, but if he
makes it till the first of March it will be a miracle."

"Has anyone ever come to visit him except me or
Amos?"

"No, I'm sorry to say, I've tried to call his two children
but they must have moved as both phone numbers we have
on file have been disconnected. The only time they have been
here was the time we admitted Epp. As far as I know he has
not received any correspondence or phone calls from them."

"Doctor Horton, when Epp passes away I want to take

care of his funeral expense and to have him buried in our family cemetery. Would you please call me when he passes on? I owe Epp more than just my ranch. I probably owe him my life as well. The least I can do is to make sure he gets a burial that a man like Epp should have."

"Ben, I will make you a promise that I will do my part. I really didn't know Epp until you had that fiasco here at the clinic. After talking to him about what happened to you I found out what a real man Epp is. A doctor is not supposed to get involved with his patients but I found out how hard life can be talking to Epp Hardin."

Ben let Amos out at the church and told him that he would pick him up in the morning; as Amos was going to spend Christmas Day with the Adams family.

Christmas wasn't the same this year as in years past, and it seems more a time of sadness than joy. Ben asked if Amos would offer a prayer.

Amos gladly did so. "We as Christians should rejoice and thank God for this is the day set aside to honor the birth of His Son and Our Saviour. Who else but our Creator would let His only Son suffer so much and sacrifice his life and shed his blood to save all of those who accept Christ as their only hope to live throughout eternity in heaven, Amen."

"Amos, how can God let things like this war happen?"

"Ben, God gave mankind a free spirit and a free mind to choose the path they take in life. God doesn't let nor make them happen; it's mankind who destroy themselves and others. God will separate the good from the bad in His own time."

Ben visited Epp twice a week as did Amos on alternating days. Each day Epp looked a little weaker and tired. During a visit he had with him in mid January, Epp said, "Ben, I'm dying a little more every day. I know my time is about all played out. I don't have a penny to my name and my two children haven't seen me or written me since I've been locked up in this place. I hate to ask you this, but please don't let the county bury me. I know it's a lot to ask but I have nowhere else to turn to."

"Epp Hardin, Amos and me and my whole crew are going to place you in Mother Earth on my ranch in our family cemetery. You will get as good if not a better burial as any good old cowboy ever had. Just tell me what kind of clothes you want and I'll see to it, even a new pair of boots if you want them."

"Ben, I don't know how to thank you. You wouldn't even let me pay you when you helped me get my cows back on my place years ago. Now here you are when I need help again. I wish there was some way to make you understand how much I appreciate you as a friend."

"Epp, you don't know how much I owe you for all you have done for me. I might have lost my ranch and be here where you are if you hadn't told me about what those three crooks were up to. You don't concern yourself about anything; I want to do all I can to see that you have nothing to worry about."

"Ben, just bury me in cowboy clothes like I've worn all my life. I would like to have my boots, hat and a blue neck scarf on when you close me up in that wooden casket. If you have an old pocket knife, stick it in my right hand pants pocket."

Ben promised Epp he would make sure that it would be exactly as he wanted it to be.

After leaving Epp, Ben went to a store that sold ranch wear and purchased just what Epp requested, including a pair of long john underwear.

Next was a stop at the local funeral parlor. This was the same one where he had arranged for his wife's funeral. Ben placed his package on the floor beside the chair that was offered him by the owner.

The undertaker asked Ben if he has another death in his family and Ben explained his promise to Epp. Ben was very detailed about what Epp wanted and to make sure it was carried out to the letter.

The undertaker told Ben that he would personally attend to the job himself and Ben could come by and make sure everything was what Epp wanted. Ben reached in his pants pocket and handed him a two bladed yellow handle stockman's pocket knife.

"This was the last thing Epp wanted, be sure it goes in the right hand pocket of his jeans."

Ben told him that the clinic would give the funeral home a call when Epp passed away.

Three days later Ben received a call from Amos telling him that Epp had left this earth to meet his Maker. Amos told Ben that he was visiting Epp when the old cowboy just took a deep sigh and closed his eyes. He said it was the most peaceful death he had ever witnessed.

Ben got Joaquin and the two cowboys to help him dig the grave the morning of the burial. It was a cold day with the wind blowing from the north.

Ben picked up Amos on his way to the funeral home. He wanted to make sure that Epp was dressed as he wanted to be for this sad send off. He was.

At two o'clock all of the hands that were employed by Ben were at the grave site. Doctor Horton stood by Ben as Amos Brown spoke in a quiet voice sending Epp Hardin into a better world. Amos asked for hats to be removed and heads bowed as he prayed for The Almighty to give Epp a place in His kingdom.

Doctor Horton reached down and picked up a handful of earth and sprinkled it on the lowered casket and told the group that Epp was one of the best men he had ever known.

The grave was covered and the crowd left. Epp Hardin was home at last.

Doctor Horton drove up to the ranch house and caught Ben before he went inside. Ben waited on the porch until the doctor asked if he might talk to Ben for a few minutes. Ben asked him to come in and have a cup of coffee.

They relaxed in the living room by the fireplace while Ruth served the steaming brew.

"Ben, I know this might seem a mite queer but I've talked with my staff and we would like to place the headstone on Epp's grave if it will be alright with you. Epp was with us for so long that my staff feels like he was part of all of us. I know how much you thought of Epp and I wouldn't want to intrude but we all feel like we owe it to him."

"Doctor, I think that you are showing an act of kindness that I wish the rest of the world could have. I think Epp would be happy if you furnished the headstone."

"Epp told me Ben, the day before he died, that all he ever was in life was a cowboy and a Texan. That's what we would like to have engraved on the stone if you agree."

"I agree but I think it should be stated as A Real Cowboy and A True Texan."

"Ben, I'll go by the stonemasons and order it this afternoon. I will tell him to make the stone out of the same color granite and the same size as the existing ones if that's ok."

"I really want to thank you and your staff for thinking of Epp, Doctor. I know Amos will want to thank you also."

The next Monday afternoon the stonemason set the stone on the concrete base that he had installed the week before. Ben walked down the slope to watch. A car was pulling up just as he got there. Doctor Horton and Amos got out and came over by Ben as they watched the mason clean the stone and said, "I knew Epp from way back and this headstone fits him to a T. I didn't ever know what happened to him after I moved down here from Sterling City. If I'd known he was at the clinic I would have visited him every week."

The doctor thanked the mason and he gathered up his tools, thanked them for thinking so much of Epp.

The stone was exactly as Ben had told the Doctor. Amos told them that if any one deserved a headstone like this one it was Epp Hardin.

The stone read Epp Hardin 1852-1942 A Real Cowboy and a True Texan.

Chapter Thirteen

Spring came on a Thursday morning and Friday afternoon it felt like summer, just typical Texas weather. Ben put a saddle on a blue roan gelding he had named Percy and rode him up to the back porch. The horse was as gentle as a puppy and would stand all day with the reins on the ground. Ben dropped the reins and went into the house and came out with Little Ben.

Maude and Ruth stood on the porch and watched as Ben wound the reins on the saddle horn and mounted Percy with the little boy in his left arm. Maude said, "Ben you be careful with that baby. If you let him get hurt I'll sick Amos on you."

Ruth only gave Ben a big smile and watched the two ride away. She knew that granddad would take the best of care of his grandson.

It was a long ride to Pepe's place and Percy needed a good workout. It gave Ben a lot of pleasure to set a saddle of a good horse and a better feeling to have Little Ben sitting in front of him. The boy was as happy as he could be. Now that warmer weather was here Ben would take him for a ride as often as he could.

Ben wanted to talk to Pepe to see when he was going to start the spring roundup. The weather was right and they needed to get it done before the thunderstorms started.

There was a lot of activity around the bunkhouse as the old and young cowboys rode up. Ben dismounted and dropped the reins on Percy and held Little Ben's hand as they walked up to Pepe. Eva spotted them and hurried to pick up the boy. Little Ben was well acquainted with the Rojas family and went willingly with Eva.

Ben thought that Pepe was already a step ahead of him on getting the roundup started. The place was alive with lunch sack cowboys stowing their gear and arguing over who was going to get the bottom bunks. Joaquin straightened them out by telling them the oldest men got first choice.

Ben and Pepe walked to the house and Eva poured the coffee and set a batch of hot doughnuts on the kitchen table. She had Little Ben wrapped in her left arm resting him on her hip. Ben wondered when Joaquin and Maria would add a sibling to the Rojas family. When it happened Eva would put the child in captivity in her house and have visitation hours for the baby's mom and dad.

Pepe told Ben that the round up would start day after tomorrow. Joaquin would have the horses in the trap and all of the equipment loaded by tomorrow and the other hands would arrive by tomorrow night. Ben told Pepe he would be there and give them a hand if they would not make fun of an old codger. Pepe told him this bunch would try to poke fun at their mother if they didn't have anyone else to pick on.

"The only trouble they have, they know that you are the boss, so I don't think they will try to put one over on you. Besides you are a better hand than any of them and they know it."

Ben mounted Percy and Eva handed the boy up along with a large sack of doughnuts. Little Ben waved bye and they headed for home.

They arrived at the back porch at dusk and Maude came down the steps to take the boy, but Little Ben turned away and held on to Ben. Ruth tried and received the same treatment. Ben dismounted leaving the boy in the saddle. He handed the sack to Maude and told her they were for Little Ben. Taking the reins, Ben led Percy to the corral, opened the gate and put him in a stall. He lifted Little Ben off, unsaddled and gave Percy a rub down and a bucket of crimped oats. Ruth and Maude stood on the porch watching as Big and Little walked hand in hand to the house.

Ruth told Maude "I wish James was here to see this."
From far away, James was wishing too.

Chapter Fourteen

Things were happening just like James had said. Ben was rationed as others, but because of his ranch supplying wool, mohair, beef and grain to the country, the shortage was not severe enough to hamper the operation of the ranch.

When Ben went to town he could see cars set on blocks with a cover over them.

Butter, sugar, lard along with other food supplies were hard to come by. Tires, tubes, oil and gasoline were almost impossible to purchase. Hard times had come to America as far as the commodities most people were use to.

The spirit of the people was at an all time high. Young men stood in long lines to volunteer to any branch of the armed services. Young women also did more than their part, not only to serve in the military but to take the place of the men who went to war.

Automobile factories built aircraft, tanks, personnel carriers and the mighty Jeep.

Every place of business that built anything worked twenty four hours a day seven days a week for the war effort.

All scrap steel, copper, brass and aluminum were in great demand. Children flattened tin cans and saved aluminum from chewing gum wrappers. Saturday matinees were offered at the movie theaters, price for admission was a dozen tin cans that were washed and flat. Only kids were admitted. There were not enough seats for any one over twelve years of age. The war effort was making Americans pull together as a one team nation.

Attendance for religious services was at an all time high. Mothers placed small banners in the windows of their homes, proudly displaying their son or daughter was serving in the military.

The government was building an Air Force Base on the

south east side of San Angelo. Anyone that wanted to work could find a job anywhere. There was always some who didn't know what work was. Wonder why?

Ben was talking with Slim Simmons at the tractor shed when a car with two men dressed in business suites pulled up. They asked if the owner was here. Ben introduced himself, and Slim, and then asked if he might help them.

The taller of the two explained who they were and said that they were with a major oil company and would like to speak to him about a lease on his property.

Slim told Ben he needed to get back to work and would see him later.

Ben asked the oil men to come in and have a cup of coffee and they could talk in the kitchen.

Ruth set the cups on the table and poured coffee and took Little Ben out on the front porch with Maude.

"Mister Adams, we would like to lease all of your land to drill for oil, as the nation needs all we can produce. We are prepared to pay you the going price for the lease for five years with a renewal clause to extend the lease if oil is discovered. We will take care of all your property, build our own roads, and put the land back to the shape it's in when we leave. We have a contract we would like for you to look over and let us know what you think. We will be back this way in a week."

Ben told them if it was not for the war he wouldn't look at it, but knowing how desperate the nation needed oil he would help any way he could.

They thanked him and told him they would see him next week.

Ben didn't even open the contract to look at it. He got on the telephone and called his old friend Judge Earl Biggs. The Judge was in court but his clerk told Ben that she would give the message to call him. Ben thanked her and hung up.

Late that afternoon Earl called Ben and asked if he could be of help. Ben told him of the oil men and the contract, and wanted to know if he knew of an honest lawyer, if there was an honest lawyer, who specialized in this field. Earl told him of an honest one in San Antonio that was the best in the business. Ben asked for his name and phone number.

Earl told him to hold on a minute and he would look it up. A minute later he told Ben the man's name and phone number and told Ben to tell the man that Judge Biggs recommended him to you and that you need to see him as soon as possible. Ben thanked Earl and told him he would buy the coffee next time he was in town.

Early the next morning Ben placed a call to Mister Simon Fry, Attorney at Law. Ben told Mister Fry what Earl asked him to say, and Simon Fry told Ben he would see him this afternoon right after lunch. Ben said he could be there.

Ben asked Maude and Ruth if they would like to go to San Antonio to shop for a while. He knew what the answer would be before he asked. Of course they would.

Fry's office was close to the Alamo and Ben told them to meet him there when they were finished. Just try to get there by dark and take care of Little Ben.

At one o'clock Ben seated himself in front of Fry's huge desk and explained about the oil company men and handed Fry the contract. Fry looked thru the document briefly and told Ben that the company was a very reliable one but the contract was all in the favor of the company and that Ben should tell them to shove it.

"Mister Adams, I've been in this oil contract business for thirty years and these people are all the same. I'm thankful that Judge Biggs asked you to call me on this. I will write you a proper contract that will be fair to both parties. How much land do you own with all the mineral rights?"

Ben told him sixty-two sections, but there were certain areas that he didn't want any drilling done on. He unrolled a map of the ranch and with each section marked one thru sixty- two. The ones marked in red could not be drilled on. Ben told him of all the water wells and windmills and he could not afford to have any of the ground water polluted. The wells were marked with an X and the depth of each one was noted beside the X. There were fifty-eight sections that could be drilled on.

"Mister Adams, these oil companies are going to get filthy rich while this war is going on. My fee to rewrite this contract will cost you seven hundred and fifty dollars. I can guarantee you that they will take the contract because I have two more oil companies that will. "

I will also have an inspector working for me that will cost you a flat fee of one hundred a month as long as there is oil production on your property. This man will make absolutely sure that the oil company will live up to the exact wording of the contract. I will have them send me a copy of all of their transitions of productions and sales. I can promise you that the price per acre lease they offered you will triple and your percentage of funds they sell the oil for will double. I will also make sure that you will control all of the natural gas."

"Mister Fry, I know why Earl sent me to you. I don't know one thing about the oil business. I would like to pay you for your fee and whatever advance you want for your inspector."

"I will accept my fee to rewrite the contract, but you will be billed each month after the man starts to work, if that is ok with you. I will mail the new contract to you in a couple of days. Here are two business cards from the two companies. If they try to make you think you are out of line on pricing your land just show them these cards."

Ben wrote him a check, thanked him with a handshake and left.

It had taken an hour to complete his business with Fry, so he started looking for Maude, Ruth and Little Ben. He found them in the second store he looked in. Maude made it plain that they had just started shopping and wasn't anywhere near ready to leave.

Little Ben reached out for his granddad to take him. Ben did. He told the ladies, we men will meet you at the car if you can find it.

Just down the street was a movie theater with a western matinee double feature playing. Ben paid for his ticket and the girl in the ticket booth said the boy could get in free. Ben found a seat and held his grandson in his lap.

The boy would point at the cowboys and clap his little hands. The movies had his full attention for the two and a half hours. Ben thought Little Ben might go to sleep but no chance with cowboys, horses, cows and six shooters blazing across the screen.

Ben found a drug store down the street with a soda fountain. The two enjoyed ice cream cones with Ben using a few napkins to keep Little Ben from getting it all over his face and shirt. As they were finishing up Maude and Ruth came and sat with them. They placed two large shopping bags in the floor and ordered ice cream floats. Ben asked if they were ready to go home and Ruth said that she wasn't, but her pocket book said she must. Maude was worn out and Ben asked if she wanted him to bring the car to her. With a frown, she politely told him she was not so old and tired that she couldn't walk that far just as easy as he could.

After stopping for supper, they arrived back at the ranch well after dark; Little Ben was ready for his bed. Ruth bathed him and after he got three good night kisses he was ready to start counting cowboys and horses.

The three adults sat at the kitchen and enjoyed a cup of coffee as Ben explained his meeting with Simon Fry. Maude asked if there was any oil to be found here. Ben told her that they would receive the lease money if they didn't find anything. He told her that she could sell the dry well holes for readymade post holes if there was no oil.

"Ben, I am not Amos Brown so don't try your tom foolery on me."

Chapter Fifteen

The oil men arrived as Ben knew they would. Wind, rain, hail or a tornado would not keep them away if the almighty dollar was to be added to their fortunes. They exited the car with smiles that would melt an eighty year old witch's heart.

Ben returned their handshakes, but not the smiles.

"Mister Adams, if you have any of that good coffee left, we sure could drink a cup. It has been a long morning and we missed our coffee, being on the road."

Ben knew that this was just a way to start their sales pitch so he invited them into the kitchen and asked Maude to serve them.

"This sure is good coffee Mister Adams and it is not often we get to visit such nice folks and get invited into their home. Well, have you had a chance to study our proposal?"

Ben placed the contract on the table that he had received from Simon Fry. "Yes, I have had a gentleman in San Antonio look it over. He asked me to let him act as my attorney and change a few items that he thought would make this contract a little more equal to both parties involved."

The man opened the contract and as he read it the other man looked over his shoulder for a half a minute and said, "Your attorney just happens to be Simon Fry I believe. Am I correct?"

"Yes, Mister Fry was recommended to me by a good friend of mine, Judge Earl Biggs. Gentlemen, I am a rancher, not a lawyer or a politician. Before I get into anything I do not know about, I have found it wise to speak to someone who is an expert in that field. It is not that I mistrust you or the company you work for, I just want to make sure I have someone that knows what I am getting into to look after my interest." Ben had placed the two business cards Fry had given him in the pages of the contract. While the man turned the pages the cards fell on the table.

The man who asked about Simon Fry picked them up and asked Ben. "Are these companies asking about your place too?"

"They have not spoken to me personally. They have talked with Simon Fry and each one has offered to use this contract and start exploration without making a visual inspection. I can't recall you looking over my ranch. I told Mister Fry that I had already talked with you two gentlemen and would not make a deal with anyone until I visited with you first."

"Mister Adams, we appreciate your consideration waiting, but this is not the way we usually do business. However as bad as the country needs oil we will make an exception in your case."

Ben thought that they wanted the dollars more than the oil they produced.

There were two contracts in the package that Fry sent to Ben. After signatures of both parties were on the contracts the two men took their copy and told Ben thanks and that they would start the drilling process as soon as they could set up the rigs.

Ben walked them to their car and bid them goodbye.

Ben returned to the kitchen to answer whatever questions Maude was ready to ask him. She would tell him that whatever she asked would be in reference to her job of keeping books for the ranch.

"Did the contracts get signed?" Was the first thing she asked.

"Yes sister, it was as easy as pie. They enjoyed your coffee so much they couldn't resist. I told them if they thought your coffee was that good they should try your biscuits. They said if they tried your cooking that they would have to get me to hire them on as cowboys."

"Ben Adams, if you had one more ounce of hot air inside of you we would see you explode like an overinflated balloon. I don't know how the world puts up with your line of bull." Ben knew the solution to slowing her down.

"Well, I was just pumping you up so we could take Ruth and Little Ben out to get a steak supper in Angelo. But if you are that all fired mad at me I guess you wouldn't want to be seen in public with me." She wasn't that mad.

They loaded up and headed for a dining out at Ben's expense. Of course Ben had to pick up his old friend Amos Brown.

It was an enjoyable meal. Buddy Rose and his wife Sue were there, and joined them. Sue fell in love with Little Ben. She told Ruth that she had never seen a child favor his daddy as much as Little Ben.

Buddy asked Ben how things were going at the ranch. Ben told him about the contract and that they should start drilling right away. Ben told him that Earl set him up with a lawyer in San Antonio by the name of Simon Fry, and he was the man who really made the deal for him.

They sat and talked after the meal over coffee. It was good to enjoy one another's company. Talk of the war was the hot topic everywhere, so it was not mentioned.

Little Ben sat like a cowboy astride his granddad's leg and watched the grown folks sip their coffee and chatter. He was only interested in playing ride 'em cowboy.

When it was time to depart, Sue told Ruth if she ever needed someone to keep Little Ben just drop him off at their house. Ruth said she would if she could ever get him away from Maude, Ben and Eva.

The night was clear and the stars shown in all their glory. Ruth watched the sky on the way home and thought of James. She missed him so much, having Little Ben was her pride and joy, but she wished and prayed that James would come home soon. His letters came almost every day, and he called as much as possible. She worried about him being shipped overseas but there was nothing she could do but pray for his safe keeping.

The oil company moved a rig into the first pasture to start drilling. They had to enter on the road west of Pepe's home. Eva knew they were coming and had no idea of what a rig looked like. The one on this truck was lying down, and she wondered how could you drill a hole with that thing?

The drilling platform was set and the derrick raised the draw works which were in place and ready. The crown block was lowered and the drill stem was drilling the rat hole. Drill pipe was on the rack and a joint was set into the rat hole. Another joint was attached to the drill stem and the drilling for the liquid gold was ready to commence. Water and slush pits had been dug and water hauled to fill the water pit. Diesel engines sent black puffs of smoke into the blue Texas sky as they were started. The noise shattered the peace and quiet and the hum of the pumps and engines would not cease until success or failure was the answer.

Every eight hours a new crew would replace the tired and dirty men that finished their shift. The work was hard, hot or freezing, dirty, and dangerous, always dirty, but the pay was what made it worthwhile.

Drill bits were worn out and all of the drill pipe was pulled from the hole and stacked on end on the work platform and leaned against the rack on the derrick. The drill bit was changed and the process was reversed as joint after joint of pipe was joined together and sent back into the hole.

The day the drilling started a dirty, banged up red Dodge pickup pulled up to the barn where Ben was working on a trailer trying to get the lights to work. A man got out and had to slam the door twice to get it closed. He was dressed in range clothes that had seen better days. He walked over to Ben and asked if he might be Ben Adams. Ben replied he was and the man shook hands and told him that he was Henry Fry. My brother Simon, that sits on his can all day, told me you were the man that was having these oil people trying to mess up your place. I was told to get up here and make them walk the line."

Ben took a liking to this long lean man who was a little older than him. He had a way of getting down to business without ruffling a man's feathers. Ben could tell right off that he could get whatever he started finished. Ben knew that Maude always had a pot of coffee on so he asked Henry if he thought he could stand a cup. "I believe I could take on a cup or two or three."

Maude watched from the kitchen window and knew what was about to take place, so she set the table with two slices of dried apple pie and two cups. Always be prepared was her motto.

Ben introduced Henry to Maude, Ruth, and Little Ben. Henry had his hat in his hand and told Maude, "Madam, if I had known Ben was going to introduce me to an angel, I would have worn my Sunday suit. I apologize for looking like a hobo who just got kicked off a train."

Maude's face had more than a little blush as she told Henry, "Sir, you have no need to apologize and all of the men around this ranch are working people. However it is nice to have a real gentleman like you to visit us."

Henry explained his job and that he would be here quite often. If the oil company moved in more rigs he may have to be here every day.

Henry and Ben finished their coffee and pie, drank another cup, and drove up to the first well being drilled. Henry looked the location over and told Ben that everthing looked in order. They walked over to the dog house and

Henry introduced Ben to one of the owners of the drilling company that contracted the work. He was very friendly, and was a working man just like the rest of his crew. He told Ben that he had known Henry for a long time and was glad to have him as the inspector for this project. After Henry was satisfied that all was well they headed back to the ranch.

Ben asked Henry to stop at Pepe's for a few minutes. Pepe was fixing a corral gate with a broken hinge when they drove up. He laid down his tools and Ben introduced him to Henry. Eva stood on the porch of the bunkhouse and told them that lunch was ready. Henry did not linger. After removing his hat and giving Eva a bow, he was ready to chow down. He told Eva that he had eaten his own cooking for so long and he had lost so much weight that he decided he would not eat any more of his own fixing. Eva put a double helping on the skinny man's plate. He ate it all. Henry dropped Ben off at the ranch house and told him that he would be back next week. He had asked Ben about Maude's husband, and Ben told him that he was only eighteen when he was killed in the first war and Maude had never remarried. Henry told Ben he was sorry to hear of her loss and that she was a very intelligent and attractive lady.

At the supper table Maude asked Ben when he was going to put the lease check in the bank.

"What check are you talking about?"

"The one you gave me when you handed me the mail three days after the contract was signed."

"I didn't even look at the mail. No one ever sends me anything but a bill and that's your department."

"Let me tell you about this check. It is made payable to Ben Adams for the lease of thirty-seven-thousand-one hundred and twenty acres of land at the price of five-dollars per acre per year. That is the total sum of one-hundred-eighty five-thousand-six- hundred dollars. I think it would be a good idea to put it in Buddy Rose's bank and start drawing interest on it, don't you?"

"I guess, if you say so sister."

Maude just shook her head and said, "Lord help us."

The trip to make the deposit was a family affair. Big, Little, Ruth and Maude stopped in front of the bank and Ben told the others to take the car and go on to get whatever they needed. He would meet them at the Texas cafe for lunch, but please just let Ruth drive. Maude gave him a you don't trust me look. He returned it with an I love you smile.

Ben stepped inside and Buddy motioned for him to come in his office. Ben took a chair and Buddy asked if this was a business or a social call. Ben said both.

Buddy smiled and said, "Let's get the business out of the way first. Ben, I have never lent you a penny. I hope you need a loan so I can make a few dollars on the interest that I can charge you."

"Well, how much are you charging on interest now days?"

"As much as I can get."

"How much are you paying to folks who put money in your bank?"

"No more than I have to."

"Buddy, when we were kids and played marbles you always came out winner when we played for keeps."

"Yes, but I always gave them back to you so I could win them again."

"Well, if I could put a little money in here for you to loan out, I figured you to be fair with a bad marble player."

Buddy laughed and told Ben he would get the best rate he could pay because he had been lending Ben's money for years to his customers that borrowed.

Ben handed Buddy the check and told him to put one-hundred-fifty-thousand in the interest bearing account and the balance in his saving and checking account.

Buddy looked at the check and said, "Ben, this is the largest check I have ever handled."

"Buddy, this is the largest one that I have ever received."

"Well, I can put it to good use and it will make you a little money to add to your savings."

"I would appreciate it if you would handle this yourself, I rather no one knew any more about my business than they already know."

Ben thanked Buddy and walked from the bank down to the Ford Auto Dealership. There was only one man that he could see in the front part of the building. It was so quiet you could hear a penny if one was dropped on the concrete floor. The man walked up to Ben and asked if he may be of service.

"Sir, I am looking for a new automobile. I thought you might have a few."

"I only have one in stock. It is a left over. I ordered it before the war started and just received it last week, as it is hard to get your left over orders delivered. I have it in the make ready area in the back if you care to look at it."

Ben said, "Let's look."

The car was a forty-one model Ford club coupe, painted a metallic green with the deluxe emblems in chrome along with both bumpers and grill. It took Ben's eye, but he made sure the salesman didn't notice. "Well, if this is the only one you have I guess I will have to take it if the price is right. How much will it take to drive it home?"

"The list price is nine hundred and forty dollars. If you pay cash I can let you have it for nine hundred even."

"Let's go up to your office and I'll pay you and tell you who to make the title out to." After they were seated Ben asked to whom he should make the check out to.

The salesman told Ben he thought he was going to pay

cash, how was he to know the check was good. Ben asked if he knew Buddy Rose. Yes, he knew Buddy.

"Then you call him and ask if this check would clear the bank."

The man called Buddy. He looked at Ben and asked, "Ben would you like to buy a Ford Dealership."

"No thanks, just the car."

Ben explained to the man how he wanted the papers made out and to have the car ready, full of gas and that he would be back in a couple of hours or so.

Ben walked to the Texas cafe and the ladies weren't there yet. He walked east toward the main part of town until he came to the saddle shop. Ben had bought several saddles and a lot of tack from Hiram Weeks, who was the owner and saddle maker. They shook hands and made small talk as Ben enjoyed the smell of leather.

"Hiram, I need a small saddle for my grandson, do you think you might find time to make one?"

"Ben, my business is a little slow since the war started. I would be happy to make the little feller a good saddle. Do you want anything special in the tooling?"

"No, nothing fancy, make it with a slick seat, not one of those padded ones that puts blisters on your rear end."

"What you want is just a first class saddle like we grew up with. These drugstore cowboys all want looks instead of comfort and service. I'll get it made and give you a call when it's ready."

Ben gave Hiram a fifty dollar bill for a deposit and told him to take care.

When he got back to the cafe he entered and found a table that would seat four and ordered a large glass of water and a cup of coffee. He could see the street and was on his second cup when he watched Ruth park in front. They came in and joined Ben. Little Ben reached for his granddad and was rescued from Aunt Maude.

They ordered and ate. Ben asked if they were finished and ready to go. They had enough of city life for the day. Ben told Ruth to drive, and Maude asked if he was afraid to let her drive. Ben told her he was not afraid, he just wanted to get home in one piece. Maude gave him a hard look but knew that he was trying to give her the same treatment she gave him. Ben told her that she had to sign some papers for him on a deal he had made at the Ford place, and then she could drive home.

Maude sat in front of the dealer as he showed where to sign. When she finished she asked, "What did I have to sign all of this for?" The dealer told her to come with him and he would explain.

They walked up to the new Ford club coupe and he handed her the keys and told her, "This is what you signed for, it's yours."

"What do you mean it is mine, I never bought a car in my life? I bet my brother Ben is trying to put something over on me. I will go chew him out right now."

When she walked back to the front of the building Ben, Ruth and Little Ben were gone, their car was gone too. The dealer handed her a note.

Sister, I told you that you could drive home, so just get in your new car and drive. Love Ben.

Maude had tears in her eyes as she and the new Ford ate up the highway to the ranch.

Chapter Sixteen

Henry Fry was almost a permanent fixture at the ranch, as the first well was producing at a steady rate. Two more rigs were brought in and were drilling on the two sections where Pepe's family lived. Eva asked Ben if she could put the cook house to work feeding the crews as long as there were no cowboys to feed. He told her to put whatever money she made in her pocket. She told him that she would buy all of the supplies, and if she made any money it would be for her grandchildren's college education, if Joaquin and Maria ever had any. They would. You could bet on it.

Henry was very intelligent and a good man. He told Ben that he lost his wife years ago in childbirth, the baby was lost also. He said it was a hard thing to live with. Ben told him about Elsie and said he felt like part of him went with her.

After Henry shared supper with them one night, Maude asked him if he would go to church with them on Sunday. Henry told her that he had not been to church since he lost his wife. She told him that it was time to put the past behind, there was no way to bring it back. He agreed to go the next Sunday.

Henry was a man of his word. He arrived at the ranch house before time to leave and had coffee with Ben. He told them that he was ashamed to drive his old pickup and would ride with them if they didn't mind. They went in Ben's car with Ben doing the driving. Maude didn't criticize Ben's driving one time. Ben hoped that Henry would ride with them every Sunday. He did. Maude was a changed person. Thank the Lord.

Henry told Ben that it was good to be getting back to church, and asked what he thought about him placing his membership here. Ben told him that the church would welcome him with open arms. Henry said that he would get it done.

The next Sunday when Brother Amos Brown gave the invitation, Henry Fry walked to the front of the building and told Amos that he wanted to become a member of the First Baptist Church of San Angelo. He told Amos of the death of his wife and child and was a member of the same faith in Midland when the tragedy happened. He had not attended church since the loss of his wife, but after visiting here he knew what he had missed.

Miss Effie put Henry Fry's name in the membership book. Once again Henry belonged.

While in church Ben looked at the seats vacated by the young men who left to fight for their country. It was a heart rendering feeling to think of the worrying and the anguish of parents and wives. He thought of Ruth and James and knew they were not the only ones that this war had hurt. He had read in the paper where P.F.C. George Pate, the young man who worked in the U.S.D.A. office, was killed in action when his Marine Company landed on the shore of an island in the South Pacific that was held by the Japanese.

About ten o'clock that night Ruth received a call from James. He was coming home on furlough and would arrive at Lackland around noon, could someone pick him up? You bet!

Maude told Ben that she would let Ruth take her new car and pick James up. They needed a little time to themselves. She and Ben could keep Little Ben.

Ben thought it was a good idea, but told her to ask Ruth. Maude talked to Ruth and she said that maybe she could get all of James's attention for a few hours.

James was not prepared to see Ruth alone. He was use to the whole welcoming committee, but he was so happy to see his wife, all other thoughts vanished.

James asked about the new Ford and Ruth told him the trick his dad played on his auntie. James told Ruth that was the way Ben told her how much he loved her.

Ruth agreed.

James called Ben and told him he needed to pick up a few things in San Antonio and that they would spend the night there and be home tomorrow afternoon. Ben told him not to hurry.

Ben had a bay pony already broken and had picked up the saddle from Hiram. He had the pony in the corral and the saddle in the barn. When he thought it was about time for James and Ruth to arrive, he brushed down the pony and saddled him up. He sat on the front porch with Little Ben in his lap watching for the green Ford. When he spotted the car top the rise, the two of them headed for the barn. Ben placed his grandson in the saddle and led the pony to the front of the house. Ben watched the pony to see if the car might spook him. It didn't.

James left the car like a shot out of a gun, and headed for his son. Little Ben reached his arms out and said daddy. James lifted him from the saddle and hugged him with tears flowing down his cheeks. It seemed that the boy had grown a foot since he had seen him last. Maude came down the steps and gave James a hug. He sat the boy back in the saddle and he returned her hug. She stepped back and said to James, "Look at your son, and you will be seeing yourself twenty two years ago."

Ben gave his son a hug, and told him welcome home.

"Dad, you are spending too much money on Little Ben and you are going to spoil him rotten."

"I'm not doing anymore for him than I did for you, so I guess you are spoiled rotten too."

Maude told James that he spoils all of his kin and

friends. Ruth said it was good to be spoiled by Ben; he was the most generous person in the world.

Maude told him that Eva was fixing a large Mexican supper to welcome him home. They expect us to be there around five this afternoon.

"Auntie, I have not had a bite of Mexican food since I left here last time. I think that I could eat it three times a day for the next month and then take a sack lunch with me when I have to start back."

When they arrived at the cookhouse Eva gave James kisses on the cheeks and hugged him. Pepe and Joaquin shook his hand, patted him on the back as did the two cowboys. James was at home again.

Henry Fry was staying in the bunkhouse with the two cowboys since there was plenty of room. Ben introduced him to James and told him of the work he was doing for the ranch. This was the first James knew about the oil contract and was proud of the way Ben handled it.

As they were talking a pickup drove up, and Ben knew the man who got out. He was the foreman for the cleanup crew for the drilling company, his name was Curtiss Harvill.

Curtiss called out to Henry."Hey you mean old man," he said with a smile, "they told me that you wanted to see me."

"I truly do you worthless bag of bones. Didn't I ask you to clean that drilling mud out of that slush pit on that first well and fill it in and reclaim the ground?"

"Henry, you have chewed my tail out so many times I'm going to buy myself a pair of cast iron underwear."

"When you do that, I'll buy myself a high powered blow torch."

"Henry, it's still too wet to dig out. I've checked that mud every day. It's going to be sometime next week before its dry enough to clean up. Is this all you wanted to chew me out about?"

"No, I just wanted to see if the company had fired you on account of how mean you are to a poor old man like me."

"I would treat you like a real human being if you would offer me a cup of coffee once in a while."

"Well, I can fix that little problem right now. Eva is standing in the cook house door waving a cup at us. If you have a quarter in your pocket, you should leave her a tip just for putting up with you. If you don't I'll loan you one."

Ben and James got a kick out of hearing these two friends humor each other.

Eva had prepared a feast to welcome James home. There was enough food to feed twice as many. Curtiss joined in like he was one of the family, just plain old Texas hospitality.

After the Adams family got back home it was past time to milk the two cows. Ben lighted a coal oil lantern and James went to give him a hand. The smells of the barn brought back memories of his childhood to James. He remembered his first try at milking, he really didn't make much head way until Ben showed him how. While Ben milked one James milked the other. He didn't know how much his dad wished that James was home to stay. James dreaded how he was going tell them that as soon as his furlough was over that he was being shipped to England.

The next morning the Adams family picked up Amos Brown for a trip to the breakfast table at the Texas cafe. Amos was happy to see James home. He told James that he prayed every day for his safe return. Maude told Amos that he wasn't the only one. We all do.

The days passed to quickly and it was about time for James to tell his loved ones of him being shipped overseas. Well just get it done.

Late that afternoon as they all sat on the front porch

James decided he had put it off as long as he could.

"I have not told any of you yet that I am going to be sent to England as soon as I return to base. I wanted to enjoy being home, and not have to worry any of you. I hope you don't think it was bad of me not to tell you any sooner, but I just didn't have the heart to do so."

Ruth replied, "James, we all knew it was going to happen sooner or later and I am glad you waited. These past days have been the happiest of my life. The only thing I dread is being away from you for so long a time. I know in my heart that God will take care of you and bring you safely home when this war is over."

Ben asked, "Son, is your entire company going?"

"Yes dad, Major Lee has been promoted to Lieutenant Colonel, and we will undergo training with the Royal Air Force in a new aircraft they have built. It is a twin engine plane constructed of plywood and is faster than any the Germans have. It is to be used both as a fighter and aerial photography aircraft. I don't know how long the training period will last, but I'm sure it will be on a hurry up basis. England is taking a pounding from the German bombers, and there is talk of some new kind of a self guided flying bomb. They want us to find and map the bases from which they are launching them.

"Daylight raids by our B-17 bombers are having an effect on the German factories, but we are also losing a lot of planes and good men. The quicker our group locates the airfields and launch sites the sooner that we can destroy them. I want you to know that my job has a certain amount of danger but nothing like our bomber crews."

Amos went with them as they all took James back to Lackland. It was the hardest goodbye for each one. Amos hugged James and told him to keep his faith in God. It would be the best protection he would ever have. Maude told him how much she loved him and she knew her prayers would be answered. Ben shook his hand and gave him a big hug and told him he loved him and how proud he was of him. Little Ben hugged his daddy's neck and received a hug in return and a big kiss. Ruth felt like she could never let James go.

Tears flowed from both as James told her how much he loved her, and for her to take care of herself and their son. She promised she would and for him to do the same.

They watched as a driver in a jeep picked James up and drove him to a C-47 twin engine plane. James entered, and a moment later waved to them from the pilot's window. The props started turning as the engines fired up and James taxied the plane to the runway. The craft sat still for a few moments then the engines came alive and the plane started rolling down the runway gaining speed. The tail lifted a little and in a moment the aircraft lifted off from Mother Earth and headed for the wild blue yonder. How long before his loved ones would see him again?

Chapter Seventeen

Back at the ranch things were never normal as before the war. Times and people changed everything that was normal. Now four rigs ran 24\7. Noise from all the machinery ran even the coyotes away. Eva told Pepe that she thought her brain was going to fall out. Pepe told her if it did fall out it was so small they would never find it. Try to hang on to it.

Pepe slept in the bunkhouse for a week. Eva told him he better get his sweet britches on or move over permanently with the cowboys. He told her to buy him two pair. She told him that her brain was larger because if it wasn't for her he would still be shearing sheep. He didn't argue.

Every well that was drilled brought forth money for the oil company and the Adams ranch. Every month Ben's royalty check was larger than the one before. The livestock had gotten use to the noise, and Eva complained no more. Work for the ranch got back on an even keel. Ben made the rounds with Pepe one day, then with Henry the next. Slim had his farming crew in high gear, and the cattle grazed around the fenced wells on the new grass planted by Curtiss and his crew.

Henry was at every location each day making sure that the oil men lived up to the strict contract written by his, sit on his butt, brother for Ben and his ranch. Henry did however, have time to stop by the ranch for coffee. Wonder why.

Buddy Rose told Ben if he kept on making so much money he would have to build a larger bank. Ben told him that he would start burying the money in a baking powder can if he did. Little Ben spent as much time with his granddad as his mother would allow. Everywhere Big went Little would try to follow. Granddad did not mind.

During a Sunday morning church service Ben noticed a slight tremor in Amos's voice as he gave his sermon. After dismissal Ben asked, "Amos, are you feeling ok? I noticed that your voice was a little shaky."

"I felt a little funny Ben, my head started spinning and I felt like my mouth was going numb. I guess I'm getting to old for my own good."

"Maybe I should take you down to the emergency room and let them check you over. It's best to find out now instead of waiting until something bad happens."

"I think I'll be ok Ben, I've never been real sick a day in my life."

"Why don't you come and have Sunday dinner with us? I'm buying."

"Well since you put it that away I better go before you change your mind." They all went.

After the meal Ben was taking Amos back to the church, when suddenly Amos just crumpled up like a wet wash cloth. Ben made a U turn and headed to the hospital as fast as he could. The attendants helped Ben get Amos into a wheel chair and into the emergency room. Maude parked the car and she, Ruth and Little Ben joined Ben in the waiting area.

After a short wait the doctor came out and told them that Amos had a light stroke. When Maude asked if he would recover, the doctor told them that he might in time, but there was the possibility that another stroke might occur at anytime. Rest with peace, quiet and therapy would be the best thing for his recovery.

Ben asked if they offered that here at the hospital. Yes it would be best to let us keep him here and watch him closely for a while.

After they were sure that Amos was in a private room and was well taken care of they drove back home. Ben called Pepe and Eva and told them of Amos. Ben could hear Eva crying in the back ground. Then he called all of the members of the church and relayed the message to them. It was a sad time for all.

Monday morning Ben visited Amos. It was hard to find a place to stand or sit as the hospital room was full of flower arrangements of all sizes shapes and a rainbow of colors. The room smelled like a florist shop. The nurse was there with Amos and told Ben that they needed another room just for the flowers. Just goes to show how a person is thought of by his friends.

After the nurse left, Ben asked Amos if he was feeling better. Amos nodded his head and tried to speak but his speech was slurred and it was hard to understand him. Ben sat by the bed and took Amos's hand. He told him not to worry that he was going to be alright in a few days. Ben told him that he shouldn't stay to long as the doctor told him that rest and quiet would help the recovery process. Ben promised to check on him every day. He did to.

After two weeks passed the doctor told Ben that Amos could be released from the hospital. Ben asked the doctor if he could recommend someone who might help watch over Amos if he was to take him home to the ranch. The doctor said that he needed to be watched at all times for a while to make sure that he didn't fall and injure himself. He told Ben he should take Amos to the clinic where he would have someone with him at all times. Ben told the doctor that Amos would feel like he had been deserted if Ben was to place him there.

"Doctor, I know this may sound strange to you but I think as much of Amos as I did my own dad. I will hire whatever private nurses it takes to take care of him and keep him in my own home."

The doctor gave Ben a list of home care nurses and told him that all of these people were qualified to do the job. He also told Ben that what he was doing for Amos would help his recovery. Just being with someone who shows love and care helps more than anything in the healing process.

Ben called Maude and told her of his intentions. She replied, "Ben, I know that this is the best thing we can do for your old friend. I will have a room ready for him by the time you arrive.

Ben helped Amos to the car and Amos asked," Where are we going?"

"Amos, where would you like to go? I think that the best place would be where you feel like you are home."

"Ben, I've never had a real home since I was a child. The only place I really cared for was being at you place. Your family is the only one I have really felt at home with."

"Well, partner that's where we are headed. Maude already has a room ready for you, and I am having round the clock nurses ready to assist you if you need anything."

"Ben, do you know how old I am?"

"Amos, when the Pilgrims landed you was standing on the rock, saying howdy y'all."

"Well Ben, I'm not quite that old but I'm getting along in years."

"Amos, age doesn't matter; the thing that matters most is life. You only have one on this earth, and we want you around here for a long time."

They helped Amos to the kitchen table instead of his room. He told Maude that the coffee that they served at the hospital was so weak it wouldn't make his kidneys operate. He had dreamed about her coffee ever since he had his last meal here. About that time Henry Fry came in and gave Amos a hug and told him how glad he was to see him. Maude gave Henry a smile as she sat the cup in front of him. Ben got his own, so much for sisterly love when Henry was around. Oh well.

Ben hired three ladies to help Amos with any need he

might have. Amos helped the nurses to know their need to be a Christian. All things that happen, happen to good of them that love the Lord. Amos knew all about it. He was still working at the only profession that he knew. Amos was happy.

Chapter Eighteen

While Amos was not capable of filling the pulpit, the elders agreed to try a new minister. They agreed to let a new one try out four Sundays in a row, and then another would take his place for four Sundays. This way they could keep the ball rolling to see if Amos would be able to return. They wanted to hold the pulpit as long as they could for their beloved minister and friend.

They were on the tenth preacher, when Ruth got a call from the Western Union office in San Angelo that there was a wire for her. She asked Ben if he would go pick it up for her. She told them she was positive that it would concern James. She did not think she could drive being so nervous. Ben was nervous too, but he wouldn't let them know it for the world. Ben would try to think of something to put his mind on except it was no use. After losing his wife he didn't know if he could stand it if James was killed in action. Ben picked up the telegram and returned home.

Ruth and Maude were standing on the porch with Amos in his wheel chair and Little Ben on his lap. Ben saw no smiles. Ruth asked Ben if he had read it. Ben told her it was addressed to her. She asked him to read it. Maude had to go find his glasses. Amos told them to bow their heads while he said a quiet prayer.

"Our Heavenly Father, You have heard our prayers for James, and our faith will not be broken. Let us read this message as you show us your protective power, Amen."

Ben got his glasses on and opened the telegram. He stared at it for a moment, and then started reading. *Ruth-James has been wounded-stop- his wounds are not life threatening-stop-letter will follow-stop- Lt. Col. Lee-stop.*

Amos quietly said, "The Lord hears and answers our prayers."

Ruth had tears running down her cheeks as she hugged Amos and told him how much he had helped her maintain her faith. Maude said, "Amos, I will never doubt your prayers again." Ben just laid his hand gently on Amos's shoulder and gave him a little squeeze. Amos smiled.

The doctor had given Amos a prescription for a blood thinning medicine and it needed refilling. Ben told the ladies that Little Ben could go and help him get the pills. Ruth smiled and told him, "Amos may not let him go."

"I already checked. Amos is taking his afternoon nap." Maude told him all he wanted to do was fill the boy up on ice cream. What's wrong with that?

At the drug store, Ben handed the empty container to the druggist, and asked if he would refill it. When he returned with the filled bottle, he said, "Ben, I know what you are doing for Brother Amos and I would like to donate these pills to show we want to help fray your expense."

"Sir, that is very kind of you but how can you stay in business if you give your stock away?"

"Ben, you're the one carrying the heavy burden, let me just lighten your load a little." Like they say the best people in the world live in west Texas. Ben thanked the druggist and paid for the ice cream, but Little Ben wanted another. Well, one more won't hurt.

Sunday morning they all got ready for church. Ruth and Little Ben rode with Maude. Henry was sitting in the back seat of Ben's car assisting Amos. Upon their arrival at church Ben and Henry helped Amos into his wheel chair and pushed him inside. Amos set in the back, with Henry seated on one side and Ben on the other. This was the first time Amos had attended, since his stroke, and the entire church body visited with him before service started. It gave him a good feeling.

The new preacher was a young man with a withered left hand and arm. Ben figured it was that way from birth. It was the reason that he had not been drafted into the service. The new preacher's first sermon was one of love thy neighbor as thyself. It was self explanatory if he had watched the members show their love for Amos.

Amos would be the last to leave the building as service was ended. He noticed as Gladys Henley and Matilda Maynard cornered the new preacher, and was telling some wild story about one of his flock. Amos had kept them from spreading wild gossip for the last few years by hearing it first, he could, as you say, cut them off at the pass, before the rest of the town had to hear another lie. He often wondered if these two old maids ever told the truth about anything or anyone.

On the way home Maude got a ticket issued by a Texas State Trooper. She was as mad as an old setting hen that had been chased off of her nest. Ben asked her what the reason for the ticket was. She told him that the officer said she was going five miles an hour over the speed limit, and she didn't have a driver's license.

"Sister, didn't you know that you had to have your license with you every time you drove any vehicle?"

"I didn't know what a license was until the officer told me about them."

"Well, if you go take a written test and a driving test and if you pass both of them you will be issued a license to drive. If you break the speed limit you will keep getting tickets. It takes a little time for some back seat drivers to catch on."

"I'll go get it done as soon as I get caught on."

Chapter Nineteen

Ruth received the letter from Lt. Col. Lee the week following the telegram, it was sent Air Mail.

Dear Mrs. Adams:

"It is my duty as James's Commanding Officer to inform you of James's condition. I am very proud of James. He was wounded in an air battle over France. Two of our aircraft was coming back to home base, when they were attacked by four M E 109 German fighters. A dog fight pursued. James' Mosquito aircraft was hit with machine gun fire from one of the enemy fighters killing the aerial photographer and wounding James.

"The cameras on both of our aircraft were on and we have the fight on film. James downed two of the German aircraft while wounded; his wing man downed the other while the fourth German fighter departed, as two against one was no contest. James landed his aircraft and had to be lifted from it.

"As I explained in my telegram his wounds are serious, but not life threatening.

"James will be in the hospital here for some time, and then transferred back to the States for a complete examination. I do not want to alarm you but, because of the type wounds he received I am positive he will receive a medical discharge.

"There is no visual change in James; all of his wounds are to his lower back and legs. He will be able to lead a normal life, and to look at him you would not know that he was ever wounded. He has steel pins in both legs and in his back as well. He will not be capable of any strenuous or heavy work.

"Mrs. Adams I want you to know that your husband is the finest young man I have ever had the pleasure to train

and work with. When this war is over, my wife and I want to spend a few days with all of you. We enjoyed our time there so much, just to be with good friendly folks."

Sincerely:

Lt. Col. Lee

Ruth read the letter three times as she sat in a rocker on the front porch. The front door opened and a nurse held to Amos's arm as he eased himself into a chair. He gave Ruth a smile and asked how she was holding up.

Ruth handed him the letter and asked him to read it and give her his thoughts. Amos unfolded the letter and read it without glasses. This amazed her, Amos was much older than Ben and his eye sight was perfect. Amos read the letter again and said to Ruth, "I know this is a hard pill to swallow, but he will be home soon and will never have to return. I think that it is a blessing in disguise. The Good Lord knows what's best for us if we put our lives and trust in Him."

The Big and Little Bens came from the horse corral and Little had to tell his mother how he rode his horse by himself. He told her that he had named his horse Peanut, and it was the best horse in the world. Oh to be a child again.

Ben asked them if they would like to go to town and have a treat at the drug store fountain. Amos said, "If you are waiting on me you're losing time."

Maude called out, "Wait for me." She beat them all to the car.

Ben assisted Amos into the front seat while the others rode in the back. Maude did not make one comment on Bens' ability to drive. Wonders never cease.

Amos was welcomed at the store by all that were there. Ben told them that this was a celebration to get Amos out of the house to sample the best store bought ice cream in town. They all enjoyed it. Little Ben had to have another. Ben got him one. It looked to good. They all had seconds.

The next afternoon Ben was in the tractor shed when a strange car drove up. Ben walked outside and watched as the four week preacher got out. "Are you Mister Ben Adams," The preacher asked.

"Yes I am. May I help you?"

"I would like to speak with you on a private matter if you don't mind."

"I'll help anyway that I can. Would you care for some coffee?"

"What I have to say will only take a few minutes. I have come to ask you to come to church Sunday morning and confess your affair that you are having with your daughter-in-law and repent."

You could have knocked Ben down with a feather. Here was a man who had preached one sermon and had been in town less than a week and was accusing him of the worst sin that he could think of. He looked the preacher in the eyes and told him,

"I will be there to make my statement, if you will answer any question that I ask you with the truth. Will you agree to that?"

"Yes I will, and I am thankful that you are man enough to see things my way." The preacher left as quickly as he could.

Ben seldom got mad about anything but he could almost pop his cork about this big lie that someone was trying to start. Then suddenly it came to him as clear as day. Gladys Henley and Matilda Maynard, the two old maids that Amos always kept under control. Ben decided that this business of them spreading gossip had gone far enough. He decided not to tell anyone or say anything about it until Sunday at church. It was time for a showdown.

The preacher arrived at church early, thinking that when Ben made his confession that he would be a sure cinch to get the position that was going to be vacated by Amos. This was a fair size church for someone as young as him to hold the full time position as minister. Time would tell.

After Sunday school and the song service, the preacher came to the pulpit feeling confident that he was in the driver's seat. He looked the crowd over and saw Ben, Amos and Henry seated as they were last week.

The preacher cleared his throat, and started speaking. "Folks, before I render the sermon, Mister Ben Adams would like to make a confession to us and to the Lord."

Ben walked to the front of the building, and asked the preacher to stand at his side. He stepped down with a smile on his face thinking that Ben needed his support.

"Preacher, I didn't tell you that I had a confession to make, but I would make a statement. Is that correct?"

"Yes, but I thought that you were going to confess and repent."

"Preacher, did you ask me if I was guilty of what you accused me of?"

"No, I just asked you to come, confess and repent and you said you would be here and make your statement. That is what I expect you to do."

"Preacher, I have nothing to repent of. Nor do I need to confess to what you have accused me of because I am not guilty of a lie that was told to you by two members of this church. You told me that you would answer any question that I asked you with the truth. Is that correct?"

The preacher visioned that the full time position was about to slip away. "Yes, that is what I told you."

"Am I correct, that two members told you this that you accused me of?"

"I am sworn to secrecy and I will not break my oath."

"Then you told me a lie when you said you would answer any question with the truth. Am I correct?"

"I will not answer that question, but will answer any one except it."

"Then I am going to name the people who told you this big lie and you are going to answer me with the truth."

The preacher felt like running to his car and skipping town faster than a bank robber.

"Mister Adams, you are asking me to involve someone that I promised not to reveal their identity."

"Preacher, you have accused me of something that is the biggest lie on earth, and you want to protect the liars and destroy the innocent. I am going to name two people that are sitting in this church building and you can shake your head yes or no, or I will have to do it for you. Do you understand that my whole family is involved in this big lie and you are trying to protect two of the devil's angels?"

There was not a rock large enough for the preacher to crawl under. He finally realized that his desire to gain a position in this church was going to ruin a good family if he did not reveal the ones who lied to him about Ben Adams.

Ben placed his hand on the preacher's shoulder and walked him to the front seat where Gladys and Matilda were sitting. Gladys was staring straight ahead at the attendance and offering bulletin board, her face was so red it looked like it was on fire. Matilda had a funeral parlor fan beating the air faster than a humming bird could flap its wings. Her mouth was closed so tight it looked like she had lock jaw.

"Preacher, these two women sitting in front of you are the two who started you on this path of destruction, are they or are they not?"

The Preacher's voice was so squeaky it sounded like a hub on an ungreased wagon axle. "Yes, these two were the ones that told me what I told you."

"Thank you for your truthful answer, now want you please have a seat, and I will turn the service back to you in a

109

moment or two."

'Sister Effie, since you are the church secretary and treasurer will you please bring the membership book from your office?"

She returned quickly with the book in hand. Ben looked at the people that he had worshipped with for so long, and said, "Friends there is a passage in the Bible that says if you are in the midst of sinners for you to come out from among them. I helped work on this church, laying the foundation, when I was a boy. I and my family have been members of this assembly from way back. It hurts me to leave here but I am going to come out from these two who have tried to start sinful rumors and gossip since they placed membership here.

"Miss Effie, could you please remove all of the pages of the membership of the Adams family and hand them to me?"

Slim Simmons stood up and said, "Miss Effie would you remove our membership while you are at it?"

Slim was followed by Buddy Rose and his wife Sue.

Judge Earl Biggs stood and spoke to the group. "You all know me and the office I hold. I do not know of what Ben has been accused of. I do know what the law can do to someone who is trying to ruin a man's character and tear apart his family. If Ben wants to file suit against these two women, he could receive a large amount of money and have them put in jail for an extended period of time, and the preacher could suffer as well as an accessory to the fact. If I was the ones who got this mess started I would seek Ben's forgiveness and leave town before dark tonight. Miss Effie, please remove our family's membership too."

One by one asked Miss Effie to remove their names. She had written down all of the member's names but three. Miss Effie stood up and said, "I am ready to remove all names from the book. After I remove mine, only Gladys

Henley and Matilda Maynard will remain. I ask of the Deacons if I might remove just the names of Gladys and Matilda, and leave them here, and take the book with us to where ever we move to?" The Deacons agreed.

As Miss Effie handed the book of membership to the Deacons, the preacher made one more try to hold on to the hope of his possible position. He stood and asked, "What if Ben Adams is guilty of the charge made against him?'

Judge Earl said, "Well preacher, let us hold court right here and now. If there is absolute proof of your charge I am sure Ben will stand for the sentence I will hand down. If he is not guilty, then you and your cohorts must take the penalty that I will place on you. Is that agreed?"

What did the three have to lose? A lot. Gladys stood and told the preacher, "You must be crazy if you think that Matilda and I are going to take the chance of losing our money and going to jail. We are guilty as sin and you know it. You can stay and make a fool of yourself but we are leaving now!"

The two old maids started for the door and Miss Effie stopped them and handed them their memberships she had removed from the book and asked, "Where might you be moving to?"

Gladys asked, "Why do you want to know?"

"Well, we would all like to pray for the Good Lord to watch over the town that has to put up with you two."

As Miss Effie was giving her goodbye speech to the old maids, the preacher slipped out the back door and was on his way to anywhere besides here, in a hurry too.

The two women were right behind him after picking up their few belongings. They didn't even think about trying to get the deposit back on their furnished apartment.

After the surrender and hasty retreat of the trouble makers, the crowd was astonished when Amos walked up the isle to the pulpit and took charge.

"Friends, I know now why the Lord let me have this stroke. I have been trying so long to make the two women who just left us, with a sour taste in their mouths, to stop trying to spread lies and gossip about everyone in this assembly. The Lord let me step out of the way and placed them in the hands of Ben Adams. He did the job better and more completely in a week that I have tried to do for years.

"We all know whatever they accused him of was a bald face lie. Let us put this episode of our lives in the Lord's sea of forgetfulness as The Lord would have us do. When they admitted of their guilt I felt that it was time for me to, as the old saying goes, get back in the saddle again. I pray that all of you will be here in the Lord's House next Sunday. Brother Earl, would you kindly dismiss with a prayer."

Earl was good at saying the last prayer. Maybe he was hungry.

Chapter Twenty

Progress was being made in the world conflict as the Allies won battle after battle in Europe. The Japanese were losing island after island in the Pacific Theater.

James was to be flown to America next month; his progress had been slow as it had taken several operations to repair the damage done to his legs and back. Ben had made flight reservations for Ruth to be at Walter Reed Hospital when James arrived.

When the day came for her departure, Ben, Maude and Little Ben drove her to the airport in Austin. She was to take a short flight to Dallas, catch a nonstop from there. They arrived early, and drove around town looking at the Capitol building and had lunch at the airport restaurant. Little Ben watched the airplanes take off and land. He told his granddad that he liked horses better. They don't get up in the air and make a lot of noise.

Ben made sure that Ruth had enough funds in her purse to fill any need she might have. She told Ben that she would give them a call as soon as she could and tell them what hotel she would be in. When it was time to board the plane they walked with her to the boarding gate where she kissed them goodbye. Little Ben watched his mother enter the aircraft, and as she turned to look back he waved to her. She threw him a kiss and took her seat. They watched as the plane departed.

It was late when Ruth arrived at her destination. She took a cab to a hotel as close to the hospital as she could find and got a room. As soon as she was settled in she gave a call home. When Maude answered Ruth said the trip was fine and gave her the name of the hotel, her room and phone number. Maude asked her to call them back and let them know how they were doing, and if they needed anything.

It was only a short walk to the hospital, and since Ruth didn't know where James was she headed to the main entrance. Inside was a sign that pointed to the information desk. At the desk she inquired of a Lieutenant James Adams. The lady at the desk told her that they just received a Captain James Adams from a flight from England. Ruth told the lady she did not know of a promotion but that must be her husband. She got the room number and directions and found that the walk to his room was farther than the walk from the hotel. My, this is an awful large building.

She knocked on the door lightly and was bid to enter. James was sitting in a wheel chair looking out the window. She walked over to him and as he looked up his face lighted up like a flood light. His arms reached for her as she folded in his embrace. No words needed to be spoken. What God has joined together let no man take apart.

James was still the same, except that his tanned face was lighter, and he had lost a few pounds. He told Ruth that he could walk a little, but the doctors told him to go slow and easy for the next few months. Questions were asked and answered. "How is our son?"

"Growing up fast, he rides Peanut beside of your dad every time he gets a chance. He asked about you, and when I told him I was going to see you he told me to bring his daddy home, and I'm going to."

Ruth told him of the stroke Amos had, and of Ben's set to with the old maids and the preacher. James laughed and told her that he was going to tell Amos that he faked the stroke just to get Ben to rescue him from the two women.

The day passed to quickly and Ruth returned to the hotel room, promising her husband she would be back early in the morning.

Ruth called home and brought them all up to date on all that she knew. She explained that James was to have a complete physical before he could be released from the hospital, and that the hospital was full of those wounded in the war. She told them that she would call and let them know when she had any information.

The next morning as she sat with James the nurse came and told James that she needed to take him to be x-rayed and would bring him back as soon as he was finished.

That afternoon two doctors entered and asked James a few questions. The doctors told them that the operations he had were doing great, and would he like to go home. James told them that if they thought he could stand the trip, he would leave right now. Both of these doctors were Army Majors and told James that they would get him and Ruth on a flight to Goodfellow Air Base in San Angelo as there was flights ferrying personnel to the new base on a daily routine.

Early the next morning Ruth and James was driven to a nearby Army Depot that was a shipping and receiving station. The doctors had given Ruth a nurse's uniform and told her to wear it as she was to be taking care of her patient, Captain Adams. Civilians were not allowed on military aircraft except on emergency conditions. This was an emergency.

James was assisted on board a C-47 and Ruth played her part as his nurse. The flight had a stopover to load some electronic supplies and refuel. While waiting, Ruth used a pay phone, and called Maude collect, telling her of their soon arrival in San Angelo at the new air base. Maude said, "We will be there waiting." They were.

The homecoming for James was a very special occasion. Ben had the entire crew that worked on the ranch busy making preparations for a barbecue that would feed a small army. He put the word out that the event was going to take place at the ranch this coming Saturday, and told all of their friends and neighbors to come. The event would start at ten in the morning and last until dark.

There was a large roofed, open wall shed that was used for hay storage on the south side of the corrals, which was to be used just in case it rained. It was a perfect place for the gathering.

Pepe and his crew butchered two steers and would cook them over an open pit next to the shed along with a couple of Spanish goats. Eva cooked up a pickup load of her fabulous doughnuts. Maude mixed up enough mixture for twenty, one and half gallon freezers, to be cranked by volunteers. She had Henry store the precious liquid in the large ice house until it was time to put it in the freezers. Wait just a minute! We only have one freezer.

"Henry where are you?" Henry came running; he thought that Maude must have her dress caught in the washing machine wringer. No thank goodness. She told Henry her problem. Henry told her that he would not do what he had to do for anyone else but her. She watched his old red pickup disappear in a cloud of dust. Henry didn't get back until the next day at noon. Maude asked what took him so long. He told her that he could only find three freezers in Angelo and, he had to go all the way to San Antonio to find the other sixteen. He told her that he had to look in a dozen stores to get them. She could have said thanks. Oh well forget it.

Ruth and Maria cooked up twenty five pounds of pinto beans and prepared two bushels of Cole slaw to be covered and set in the ice house with Maude's ice cream mix. Two fifty five gallon barrels of ice tea were stored there too, one sweet the other with no sugar. Give e'm a choice. Joaquin and the cowboys had ten gallons of their not real hot barbecue sauce mixed up. Maude told Henry that he was going to have to help her bake a bunch of loaves of sourdough bread. Go wash your hands first Henry. Yes madam.

Bill Higgenbottom called and told Maude that they were bringing fifty pounds of potato salad.

Amos thought he had the best job of all. He told Ruth that he would watch over Little Ben. It took all of five minutes for him to call for help. James, Ruth and Ben answered the call of distress. Amos told them that the boy left him behind like a bullet leaving the barrel of a rifle, and he lost sight of him. Ben told Amos to try and keep James out of trouble, and he would take care of the runaway bullet.

Ben knew where to go. He headed straight to Peanut's stall. Sure enough the boy was setting on the top rail petting his pony on the neck. "Want to go riding granddad?"

"Not today partner, you have got to help me keep an eye on things."

"Which eye do you want me to use?" Kids! You can't help but love them. They had all things prepared by late Friday afternoon. Pepe, Joaquin and the two cowpokes agreed to take shifts during the night to barbecue the steers and would do the goats early in the morning. Slim and Betty was going to fix the corn on the cob early also.

Ten o'clock was too late for Earl and Buddy; they got to the ranch with their wives before eight. You might know ten was too late to get started without Maude's coffee.

By ten, there were more people there than you could count. Ben asked Miss Effie if she could try to make a guess as to how many there were. She was good at counting the members at church, she told Ben, and yes I can do it.

Amos finally called the crowd to the shed where they were going to eat. He asked for a moment of silence.

"My friends, we are all gathered here to welcome one of our service men home from the war. James Adams was severely wounded in an air battle over France while flying a mission to gather intelligence over Germany. The man next to him, the photographer, was killed instantly. James was hit through his legs and lower back.

"With his injuries, he still managed to shoot down two of the enemy as his wing man got another. James managed to land the aircraft safely in England. By the grace of The Lord, he has returned safely to us. Let us thank The Lord for his safe return and for the meal we are about to enjoy."

As the crowd all removed their hats and bowed their heads, Amos offered the prayer and the food started disappearing.

It was a time of fellowship. With the war going and so much turmoil in the world it was good to let the rest of the world stop for a day.

James felt like his right hand and arm would fall off from all the handshakes he had received. When someone asked how it felt to be a hero, he told them that he was not a hero, just another American trying to do his job.

Dark started settling in, and what was left of the crowd thanked the Adams family and crew for such a swell time and the good eats.

Chapter Twenty One

It was graduation time at Baylor University for the twins. The family had received their invitation and plans were made for the event.

Ruth called, and made reservations for two nights at a downtown hotel in Waco.

They left the ranch mid-morning, the day before the grand event. Ben stopped in Brownwood for a good lunch at a cafeteria, just before where the circle was, dividing the roads in different directions. He told them that he had seen flood water nearly waist deep in this area when the Pecan Bayou was on a big rise.

It was late afternoon when they arrived in Waco. They unloaded at the hotel and called the twins and asked them to join the family for supper.

After the meal they all sat in the suite and visited with Marlene and Arlene. They didn't get to see the twins to often since they were in college for the last four years. James asked if they had made any plans as what the future held for them.

Arlene, being the spokesperson of the two replied, "Yes, we have thought a lot about what we want to do. We both have a degree in marketing and we want to open a very upscale ladies store in Dallas. We have only one slight problem, the method of funding the project."

Only Ben and Maude knew the financial status of the ranch accounts. Ben asked, "Well kids how much funding are you talking about?"

"During our class, we had to make a complete estimate of cost on what kind of store we needed, and the right location. Then, how much would our beginning inventory cost. Then, how much our overhead cost would be. Also we would need a set aside fund for shelving, hanging racks, clothes hangers, and advertising. We need to set aside funds for the first three month rent and utility cost as well as insurance. The total sum comes to eighty thousand dollars. We could get a loan for half that amount if we had the other half."

Ben told them that was a lot of money to loose and pay back if they couldn't make a go of the business.

"Daddy, we have done a lot of research, and have made several trips to Dallas to see every ladies store in town. Most of them are all alike. The way Dallas is growing, there is a need for a nice store that handles the best quality merchandise and a complete stock of ladies wearing apparel for a city the size of Dallas."

After a while the twins asked Ruth and James if they would like to see some of sights around town. They could show them some of the things that set Waco apart from the average Texas town, like the first toll bridge in the country and the Texas Ranger Museum.

"Let's go before it's too late. Little Ben do you want to go?"

"Yes, I go with my daddy."

After the crew had left, Maude asked Ben what he thought about the idea the twins had about putting the store in Dallas.

"I don't know one thing about upscale or downscale ladies wear. If it was horses, cows, sheep or goats I might be able to give them some advice. What do you think about it sister?"

"Ben, I think it's a great idea. I wish we had an upscale shop like that in Angelo, but there aren't enough people to support one yet. Have you thought about what you are going to give the girls for a graduation present?"

"I had no idea I was supposed to give them a present. I didn't give one to James. If Elsie was still with me she would have taken care of things like that. I'm not very in the know about things that don't pertain to ranch life. You need to help me along in these matters sister."

"Well Ben, you know that the ranch is very well off as far as money is concerned. You could buy something, or give these children a half of a million dollars apiece and never miss it. What good is the money if you don't use it to help someone you love or someone who is in need?"

"Sister, money is one thing I hardly ever think of. All I know is what our daddy taught us as kids. Remember, he always said that if we watched the pennies, nickels, and dimes, that the dollars would take care of themselves. I guess I never thought about what a person could do with a lot of money if they had it. I always had the idea that if a person could stay out of debt and raise his family with the necessities of a good life was all he could hope for.

"I wouldn't want to give them a half a million. They need to start at the bottom and work their way up the ladder. What if we gave them fifty thousand each and do the same for James? Then if they got in trouble, that would teach them a good lesson. We could always bail them out. What do you think Ruth would think?"

"Ben, Ruth is the most level headed and lovable woman that I've ever known. She is the best thing that ever happened to James and the best daughter-in-law you could ever hope for."

"Well, what do you think if, when we get home, I have a cashier's check made out to all three of them for fifty thousand dollars each, and tell them to do as they need with the money?"

"I think that would be a good thing for you to do."

After the graduation was over, they all went out to celebrate the twin's victory over the four years of learning. It was a great dinner and when they were enjoying dessert, Ben asked the girls if they wanted to spend a week back at the ranch, and he would help them make their plans for the venture into the high dollar ladies apparel business. "I don't know how much help I might be, but we have not seen much of you in the last four years and we would love for you to spend some time with us."

"That's what we planned to do, but we may be there longer than a week. We have a lot of thinking and planning to do, and try to figure some way to raise the funds we need to get started in our business. In fact we may wind up being two old maids and never leave the ranch."

Ruth spoke in a quiet voice, "Ladies, you get that thought out of your mind. My parents left me a little money and I think we can do anything, if we want to bad enough. After we get home we will get our heads together and come up with a game plan that no banker could resist. I would be more than happy to assist you in this endeavor because I know that this is something that will be a success. You two can accomplish anything if you set your minds to the task."

The next morning they all helped the girls clean out their dorm and load it in both cars. The twins asked Ruth to ride with them and start figuring out a way to get their idea on the road. She agreed.

As they were driving home James asked Ben, "Dad, what do you think about Ruth wanting to help the twins?'

"I think it's very generous of her. What do you think?"

"Well, the money her parents left her is not nearly the amount that they are going to need to go to the banker with. I have saved most of my pay from the military, but it won't be near what they need. I think that the twins will be very successful in what they want to do. They are hard workers and I hate to see them not have the chance to at least give it a try."

"Well son, if I was you I would not be concerned about it. Your aunt Maude and I have a little surprise for the three of you when we get home."

They arrived home right at lunch time. Maude and Ruth told them to unpack while they fixed something to eat. Ben told them that he had a little personal business to take care of and for them to go ahead and eat. He changed into his everyday clothes, and got his old pickup out of the shed, and headed for town.

James asked, "Wonder where dad is headed to? He must want to check with Slim about something."

Maude told him he put on his old work clothes so it must not be anything but some kind of dirty work; far from it.

Ben entered the bank and stepped into Buddy's office. Buddy was lying back in his big overstuffed chair taking his afternoon nap. Ben sat down in the borrowers chair in front of the desk and started whistling. It took Buddy a few seconds to come alive. When he did his facial expression was that of a child caught with his hand in the cookie jar. Ben gave him a smile and asked him if he was overworked. Buddy told him that next time he had better knock before he slipped in. Ben told him that he would douse him with a bucket of cold water if he caught him asleep again.

"Well old friend, is this another social call?"

"Nope, I need a little of my money that you are getting rich on."

"I wish I was just making enough to pay my bills. How much do you need?"   "

Ben told him. Buddy said, "I got It all loaned out, how do you expect me to keep this bank open if I don't.?"

"Well I guess you will have to unloan some of it, and try to do a little work and not be sleeping on the job."

"Well if you won't tell anyone you caught me snoozing I will see if I can rake up that little bit you need."

"Make out three cashier's checks for fifty-thousand

each to each one of my kids. This is what I'm going to give them to start their way into the world on their own."

"Ben, don't you wish we could have had a sum like that to start with?"

"No, if we had a handout we wouldn't be where we are today. When you have to scratch and claw to make it, then you appreciate it. If your daddy hadn't made you work as a janitor in this bank, all during your days in high school, you wouldn't have known where to find the front door in this bank."

"You are right Ben; we can spoil our kids by not letting them know that they need to earn their own way."

When Ben returned home he parked the pickup in one of the sheds, and picked up the two milk buckets from the back porch. The two Jersey milk cows were ready to disperse their product in exchange for the feed they were to receive. Kinda' like a man doing his labor for a little payola. Ben carried the milk to the kitchen where he strained it thru the strainer cloth and put the finished product in the icebox.

The family was in the big living room talking about who knows what, when Ben told them that he had to check with Pepe. When he got back they would go to town and pick Amos up and have supper wherever they wanted to. Be sure to call Amos and tell him to be ready. Little Ben jumped off of his daddy's knee and took off after Ben. "Hey son, where do you think you are going?"

"To help granddad keep my eye on things."

Eva had to spoil the boy again with her ever present doughnuts. While she and the boy sat at the table eating a few with a cold glass of milk, Ben and Pepe discussed the work and whatever else needed to be done.

When it was time to leave, Little Ben climbed into the pickup with his ever take home sack of you know what's.

Ben showered, shaved and dressed and they were ready

for the night on the town. It usually lasted about an hour. The women folks were going to take Maude's car and were about to load up when Henry arrived all dressed up. Is he sick or something? No. He was going to ask Maude if she would like to go out to eat.

"I'm going Henry; you can ride with the men. We have important things to talk about."

Henry had important things to talk to Maude about too, but that could wait.

Amos was ready and raring when they stopped to pick him up. "Where are we going?" he asked. Everyone was ready to eat but no one knew where. After finally chasing the female gender down, they all voted for the Steak House. Henry didn't care, as long as he got something to eat, and soon.

It was a most enjoyable meal, as the twins were the center of attraction. They had been away so long everyone they knew had to make them welcome, more especially the girls with whom they were in high school with.

They dropped Amos off at the parsonage and headed home. Maude already had a pot of coffee going and Ruth was placing the cups on the kitchen table.

Ben thought how good it could be, if Elsie was only here to be with them. But as Amos had said let the past be the past. Henry finished his second cup, and told them goodnight, as he had to go to San Antonio early in the morning to file the production reports with his brother.

It was awkward for Ben to know how to start telling his children about the gifts he should have already given them. Maude got him started on the right track.

"We want you all to know that you shouldn't feel bad at your father for forgetting you at graduation time. James, your mother was dying at the time you were finishing and we could not even think about leaving her. We decided to wait until you returned from the service where we could have all of you together to present the three of you with your gifts."

"Ben, will you pass each one of them an envelope please."

There were names on all of the three envelopes. Ben wanted each one to open the others so they would know that they all got the same. He handed Marlene's to James and the one for James to Arlene and hers to her sister.

Ben told them if the one they got wasn't theirs to exchange it for their own. All three of them sat there with their mouths open not knowing what to say.

James, being the most mature, tried to give his check back to Ben. No way. "Son, I am thankful that Maude and I can do this, for you are my children and Maude's nephew and nieces and we treasure the three of you more than anything else on earth."

Ruth got up from the table and walked over to Ben with tears in her eyes and told him, "I want you and Maude to know that I think that you are the best two human beings in the whole world. I have tried so hard to figure out some way to get the girls started in their dream store that they have studied and worked so hard on. You will not be disappointed in your two daughters Ben. I know they have what it takes to be successful."

She gave Ben and Maude a hug and told them she loved them. The twins followed Ruth's example. Little Ben told them that he loved them too. "So does my daddy." James really did.

Chapter Twenty Two

The twins stayed a month, drawing floor layouts, wall shelving, shoe displays, where to place outer wear, and under garments. Auntie, what do you think about this? Ruth what do you think about that. Plan, plan, plan, change this, change that. What if we can't find a building the size to fit our floor plan? What this, what that?

Finally with three different layouts they called it quits. Thank heaven. Ben knew it was easier and a lot quicker to mark and brand a thousand calves than try to open an upscale ladies store.

With their car loaded and their plans ready to be put to use, they were off to make their fortune. Look out Big D, here we come. Every one kissed them bye and wished them the best of luck, and if they needed help just call.

The home folks hated to see them leave. The time that they had spent with them was the longest since they left for college.

Captain James Adams received a letter from the Army Air Force telling him to report to Lackland Air Base on the tenth of the month. James told Ruth that they would give him another physical, and as the doctors at Walter Reed had told him that he would receive a medical discharge. They told him he would receive a disability payment from the government for the rest of his life.

Ruth made the trip with James, as Little Ben wanted to stay with his granddad and help see to the cows.

James reported in, and was taken to the base hospital where the doctor gave him a routine exam. The doctor explained to him that he had his complete medical file, and with other doctors had studied it very carefully. "Captain, if you do not take caution and try to really take care of yourself you could be a cripple the rest of your life. The lower part of your body is held together with wire and steel pins. It is a miracle that you are walking. You are to report now to the Commanding Officer. Remember, take care of yourself.

Ruth waited outside of the C.O.'s office as James stood at attention and saluted his superior. The C.O. returned the salute, and told James to ask Ruth to join them.

"Captain Adams and Mrs. Adams, this is going to be a very unmilitary meeting. I have your complete set of records in my file, and have read them very carefully. Captain, you are a very lucky man to be alive. Your actions on your last mission were flown in the most heavily defended part of Europe. The film that you returned has changed the course of the war. Your Company C.O. speaks very highly of you and, your record speaks for itself. It gives me great pleasure to award you the Distinguished Flying Cross and the Purple Heart for your service to your country. This will be the last day of you in the uniform of the country that you have so valiantly served. You have been given an Honorable Medical Discharge due to the wounds you have received in the defense of your country.

The C.O. stood, as did James and returned the Officers salute. "James Adams, may I shake your hand and tell you how proud we are of you?"

"Sir, it is I, who thanks my country for giving me men like you to serve under."

Returning home, Ruth read through the records in James's file. Reading all of the medical reports, she knew that James could never do any kind of outdoor work. This was going to be a hard pill for him to swallow. She knew how much he loved the ranch and the outdoors. She was so thankful that he was home to stay, and she must not let him get into a state of depression because of his wounds.

Ben, Amos and Maude would have to help her. They needed to get him interested in something that he would enjoy and keep his mind occupied.

Ruth could feel and see the disappointment in James as the days passed. Little Ben asked if his daddy would go riding the horses with him. It is difficult for a child who has never felt pain to understand the agony that James has suffered. Ruth tried to tell him how bad his father had been wounded, but the boy could not comprehend. Finally she asked James and Little Ben to come into their bed room.

"James, I know how much you want to do things that you can't. I'm asking you to let me show our son, and explain why you are unable to do a lot of things with him. Would you please undress down to your shorts, and let us show him why. Then he will understand."

James complied, and Ruth told in detail of how the enemy airplanes shot the bullets that hurt his dad. The boy ran his little fingers along the scars and felt where the hundreds of stitches had been removed. Tears came into his eyes as he told his dad that he knew now why he couldn't do a lot of things. He hugged his dad's neck, and told him that he loved him.

When they were alone, James told Ruth that she had a way of understanding things, and how to overcome a problem better than Amos.

"No. Not near as well as our pastor and friend."

Ruth asked James to come and sit on the porch a while with her.

"James, I don't want you to think that I am trying to run your life. I want more than anything else for you to be happy and content. If I may help you to achieve whatever you want to do just open the door to your heart and let me in."

"Honey, I love you and our son more than anything in this world. You know that. I feel like half a man, and I know that you want to help me. I just don't know what to do or where to turn. I feel like a broken down bum with us living here with dad. I wanted so much to be dad's right hand man on the ranch. Now look at me, I can't even ride a horse. It makes me feel guilty not being able to pay my own way."

"Well, since you can't be a cowboy, let's try to think of something else that you would like, and are able to do."

"I sure don't want to go to work for my twin sisters selling ladies dresses in Dallas."

Ruth laughed and told him she wouldn't want him to even think of a profession like that. Ben, Maude and Little Ben came and sat with them, enjoying the cool shade. Ben and Maude could also feel the hurt in James. Ben wanted to talk to him about what he might do to help, but didn't know how to start. Maybe, just maybe, Henry will come to the rescue.

The next evening, just before supper, Henry and his old beat up red truck pulled up. The slam the door twice didn't work, it took another try. Maude must have been expecting him, as she had a place set for the tall, lanky, get'er done man.

After the meal was finished, the dishes were washed, dried and put away. Henry was good at drying the dishes. He asked James if he might talk to him for a few minutes.

You just couldn't refuse Henry.

James asked if he would like to sit on the porch where it was cooler. Henry said that would be fine.

"James, I am in need of some real good honest intelligent help. I don't know what you have in mind to do, but I would like to make you a proposition, if you care to listen."

"Henry, you must know that my physical condition will not let me do the things I would like to do. I cannot let you put a cripple on your payroll that is worthless."

"If I thought for one second that you were worthless, I wouldn't be sitting here now. I'm not looking for a roustabout or a pumper; I'm in need of a man to take charge of my business. James, this job that I have is just the way to get me in contact with people where the real money is made. I have been in the oil business all my adult life, and have been buying up small leases for years. Some of the land I purchased instead of leasing. I have enough property that I own or lease to drill several wells on. I need someone who can, with the aid of a good secretary, open up an office in Angelo and take care of all the paper work and the phones while I run the field work. James, I have almost a million dollars in the bank to use to do whatever needs to be done. While this war is going on I think we could make us enough money to retire on."

"Henry, I would love to give it a try, but I can't accept a salary that I could retire on. That's not the way I've been raised. I will give it a try, and accept no salary in as far as a payroll check, but stock in your company. I have my disability payment that is more than enough for us to live on and I have no debts. If you are willing to try me on that basis I will go to work for you."

"Can you start in the morning?"

"I could have started last week."

A handshake sealed the deal. "Oh, by the way, do you think Ruth would like to work as your secretary? I know we could pay her a salary." She would love to.

James told Ruth of her employment that Henry wanted her to help him with.

"What are we going to do with our son? We can't expect your dad and aunt to keep him. I'm not going to burden them with a go getter like Little Ben. He would run them ragged the first day. I guess we could find a day school for him. He's old enough to start learning what the first grade will be like. I know it will break his little heart when we move to town, and he is separated from Peanut. Have you said anything to your dad and aunt about what Henry has offered you?"

"No, I guess we had better go tell them now, as we are to be on the job in the morning." Henry doesn't fool around.

Telling Ben and Maude wasn't an easy chore. Maude had a conniption fit. "You all can't do this to me. After all the worry and praying that I have been doing, you can't just jump up and leave us like this. I want stand for it. I'll take Little Ben and run away before I'll let him go to one of those blasted unclean, rundown day care centers. He could catch any kind of a germ there that would give him no telling what." Maude could put her foot down, hard too.

Ben didn't have the anger that sister carried around on her shoulder. "Well, I sure don't see any need for you to have to do all of this moving, and changing your lives all around just to go to town to go to work. We've got plenty of room in this big old house and I don't think either one of you would get lost driving to town five days a week. Just think about having to listen to all of that noise all the time, and smelling of the dirty air for twenty four hours a day. That ought to be enough to make you want to stay home where you belong. Besides if you move to town, Maude and I will be in your office every day to see you."

About that time they heard someone slam a door three times, and then heard footsteps on the back porch. Maude called out "Come on out to the front porch Henry."

"How did you know it was me?"

"I didn't have to guess."

Maude lit in on poor old Henry. "How come you want James to move his family to town? Don't you have any respect at all for me and Ben? I thought you were a decent sort of fellow Henry and now you pull this stunt. After all the coffee, eats and friendship that I have shown you, I can now see you for what you really are."

"Do you want me to pour cold water on you to get you cooled off before you have a heart attack? You are wound up like a broken spring pocket watch. It's a good thing I stopped by or they would be hauling you to the hospital. Merciful heavens, I always figured you to be a woman of a sound mind and an even temper. I am usually a pretty good judge of a person's character but I guess I'd better quit judging.

"I want all of you to know that I never asked anyone to move anywhere. I have offered James and Ruth a position in a company I am starting up capable of making a sound profit. They have accepted the offer and are ready to start to work. That's all I'm guilty of. Now if you will pardon my intrusion I'll be on my way. I just wanted to leave this packet with my new partners."

Maude sat with her mouth open, and was shocked at Henry laying the law down to her. By the time he reached the back door, she was on her feet calling, "Henry, wait a minute, please Henry I want to apologize for me being such a you know what, please wait."

Henry waited. Maude caught him by the arm, and with tears running down her cheeks, told him what a fool she had been, and asked for him to please forgive her. He did of course. Maude asked if he would please come back on the porch with her. She told the others how sorry she was to act like she owned them lock, stock and barrel. Henry came back. Maude apologized. They were friends again.

Ben asked, "Why don't you get your business all set up before you make any decisions on what to do next? It's always better to bait the hook before you try to catch the fish."

Henry replied, "I can't see any need in you two even thinking about moving to town at all. Ruth won't need to come to work for a while. We have got to find an office, buy whatever furnishings we need, and get the phones connected up. This kind of business won't require both of you to be there all the time anyway. I would give anything to live as you folks do. Just look at Little Ben, he is the happiest most down to earth boy I have ever seen. If you move him to town it would break his heart."

"Henry, I must apologize to you once again. I never knew you were thinking the same as I was about this family."

There was a lot Maude didn't know about Henry's thinking.

The next morning James and Henry drove to San Antonio, to pay Simon Fry a visit. Henry explained to his, sit on your can, brother what they were going to do. Simon noted the information on a tablet and told them that he would draw up the papers for the corporation, and call them when they were to be signed and filed.

Henry asked his brother, "How much are you going to charge us for your time and effort?"

"How much can you afford?"

"Not much."

"Well, I won't charge you much. Maybe I can talk you into buying my lunch if you ever have enough money."

"I bought last time, but I still love you brother."

"I love you too Henry."

Driving back, James asked Henry if they were only going to be a drilling company. Henry said that was all that he had in mind. He asked James if he had any other idea of how to combine anything else that would help offset the cost, and gain income when there was less demand for their drilling services. James told him that all pumping wells had break downs at one time or another and someone had to pull and repair them. Henry told James that was the reason that he wanted him for a partner.

"You've got a good head on you James. What we need to do is buy us a pulling unit and start it working as soon as possible. When our own wells need repair we would have less expense, as we could repair them with our own rig. By the way what are we going to name our company?"

James, knowing how fond Henry was of Maude, asked him, "Henry why don't you ask Aunt Maude to pick out a name?"

"Aw, she would more than likely want to call it Buttermilk Oil or Peaches Petroleum. I guess it wouldn't hurt to give her a try, we could always tell her it was names already in use. I know that it might be a lie, but I think the Good Lord would forgive us. He might be embarrassed a little too."

That night after supper was over; they sat around the kitchen table discussing the new company they were forming. Henry asked Maude if she could think up a proper name to use. Henry was ready to think of some reason to let her know it wouldn't work. "Well Henry, if it was my choice, I would name it Wes Tex Petroleum and Service Company, Inc."

Henry wanted to shout, he couldn't believe it. "Well, I'll call Simon in the morning and let him know, if that's alright with James and Ruth." It was.

The three of them located a new building, with an office and a large warehouse on ten acres just north of town on the Sterling City highway, not far from the road that turned off to go to the ranch. Henry told the owner that the rent was too high.

"I might as well build our own or buy this one at the rate you're asking. How much would you take for it if you wanted to sell?" The owner told him what he was asking. Henry asked him where the gold mine was. What gold mine? "At the price you want there must be a gold mine somewhere on the property." Ruth was embarrassed. James was watching Henry at his very best trying to save every dollar that he could. Well if you think it's too much, what will you give me? Henry offered the man one half of what he was asking. The man shook his head and offered it to them for twenty percent less than his asking price.

Henry said, "Let's go sign the papers."

They did.

On the way to the bank to pay the man James said to Henry, "If Ruth and I are going to be partners in this business we are going to pay half of the cost of the property. We may not have the funds to pay cash for everything we need, but I can borrow enough to make sure we hold up our part of the partnership."

"Partner, you and Ruth don't need to borrow anything. Let me pay for whatever else we are going to need, and when we start making money you two can pay me back whatever and whenever you want to. Money really doesn't mean that much to me, it's just the challenge to try to make it."

The days passed quickly as the office was furnished with furniture, filing cabinets and everything else required for starting operations. Phones were put into working order and paper towels and tissue paper were in their holders in the rest rooms. Ben, Maude and Little Ben stopped by to see if all passed Maude's inspection. "Ruth, you need to place some plants and flowers in the reception area, and hang a curtain on the front window. That would brighten the place up a little."

"I guess it would. I'll get it done tomorrow."

"Come and go with me now Ruth if you're not too busy and I'll help you pick them out." Ruth went. Henry was happy.

The next morning Henry was at the ranch before breakfast time. Maude set a plate for him. Henry didn't refuse it. Maude knew he wouldn't. He told them the reason he was early that he wanted James to go on a call for the company with him. After breakfast the two headed for Pepe's. As they drove up to the cookhouse the graveyard crew was leaving after chowing down on Eva's cooking. Henry called Curtiss Harvill to stay and have a cup of coffee with them. When the three were alone sipping their coffee, Henry asked, "Curtiss how much longer have you got on this location?"

"We are on number fifty-eight now, and should set the casing, and put a pump jack on it by the end of the week. Henry, this is the only location that I've been on that every hole that was drilled was a producer. There is no telling how much oil is held in this reserve."

"Curtiss, where are you going after finishing up here?"

"The company wants to send me to do some offshore work, but I'm not too happy to leave my family. They pay a little more for that type of work but it has a lot of draw backs."

"Would you consider coming to work for Wes Tex, if the pay was better and you could be home almost every night?"

"I've never heard of Wes Tex. Is a new outfit around here?"

"Well, it may be a new company but there is an old codger and two more partners involved that have the funds and the brains to make it the best company that you will ever have the privilege to work for."

"I'll bet a hundred dollar bill that I'm speaking to the old codger, and looking at one of the ones with brains."

"I won't call your bet."

"Henry, I will have to give my two weeks' notice, and it will take me and my crew that long to clean up the last location and reclaim the ground. Can you wait that long?"

"That would work out just fine. If you run on to a good reliable roustabout crew for a pulling unit, give them the word that we are hiring. We are fixing to buy a new unit and put it to work as soon as we can. We are looking for a good rotary rig that can go deep hole also. If you hear of anything for sale let us know."

"I heard that the contractor that has the contract here wants to sell the last big rig he purchased because he can't find a driller that can operate it. I don't know what he paid for it but it's been setting in his yard ever since he bought it. I'll feel him out if you want me to. I don't know how he is going to feel about me turning in my time but I may be doing him a favor if you buy his new rig."

"Feel him out Curtiss, if he gets mad about you leaving him and sends you home, just consider yourself on our payroll that much quicker."

The deal was sealed with a handshake between the three of them.

Three days later the company was the owners of a brand new pulling unit with all of the tools and attachments to put it into operation. As the three of them were admiring the piece of equipment, a pickup stopped in front of their new office. Ruth told them she had better go see if the man was a new customer, a salesman or a bill collector.

"May I help you sir?"

"Yes madam, I'm looking for Henry Fry. I understand that he is one of the partners in this new business. Is he around by chance?"

"Yes, he is out in the yard with my husband looking at a new pulling unit that we have just purchased. You may go out and visit with him if you like, or I will call him in."

"If you don't mind I would like to see the new unit myself. I have never laid my eyes on a brand new one. The only ones I have seen were so dirty you would think they were a hundred years old." The man made his way to where Henry and James were admiring the unit.

Henry heard the approaching footsteps on the gravel and turned to see who was coming. "Well, look what the cat's drug up; I'll swear if it's not my old friend Phil Carter. James, I want you to shake hands with Phil. He knows more about the oil business than the best seismograph crew in this part of the country. Phil this young man is James Adams; we are partners in this new business." James shook hands with Phil, and told him any friend of Henry's had to be a good man.

"Henry, this is the first brand new unit I have ever seen. I hope you take the time to keep it looking like this. It would be a shame if it turned out to look like that old beat up pickup that you run around in."

"Well, if you think you can keep it in top condition, why don't you take the job as boss of it? We are looking for a man that can get himself up a good crew and put it to work."

"The reason I came by was that Curtiss told me you were buying a new unit. I had my doubts about it being new since you won't buy yourself a decent looking pickup. I guess you have decided that if you were to try to operate it yourself it would look like your truck in about a week. I guess I had better let you talk me into working for you so people won't talk about this unit like they do your truck."

James couldn't suppress a laugh. "Phil, you have got Henry pegged to a tee. If you want to take charge of this unit you are on the payroll as of now."

"Henry, you ought to be thankful that you have a partner with foresight to offer me the job, so I can keep this unit from looking like that old beat up truck."

"Well Phil, since you're being paid where is the rest of your crew?"

"I told them to wait for me at the coffee shop, that it might take me at least fifteen minutes to make you see the light. I promised them that I would bring you down and let you buy us all a round of coffee. We better hurry as my time is almost up."

The three made it with a minute to spare, and were introduced to the two that were waiting.

Phil told them that the company that he had been working for was losing their customers because their units were so old that they kept them in the shop more than in the field.

"We miss so much work, that when Curtiss told me to see you I knew that you were the man to get the job done, and keep your customers happy. I called a couple of the companies and told them that I was going to change jobs. I told them that I would appreciate it if they weren't satisfied with the company I quit, just give Wes Tex a try and let us prove ourselves. We have three wells to pull that are waiting on us. I would like to take the new unit out to the location now and be ready to start early in the morning."

Ruth, James and Henry watched as Phil and his crew pulled out of the Wes Tex yard headed for their first account to put in the ledger.

It took Henry a week to get the owners of the deep hole rig to sell at the price that he would pay. After hiring a driller that Henry had worked with for years, he told him that as soon as he could get a complete crew together he would have the drilling rig on location and set up ready to go. Curtiss came to work and relieved Henry of a lot of the work load that he had been carrying.

The location was in the northwest part of Crockett County, near the Pecos River. Henry had purchased this section of land twenty years ago, with all mineral rights. He was banking on hitting a very strong well as he had worked in this area, and knew it well.

The driller with all of the crews hired, cranked the new equipment up, and Wes Tex number one was waiting to be discovered.

Weeks passed and the hole got deeper and as some of the workers had doubts; Henry told them to have faith. Henry had to have it. Then about mid morning the next day the driller felt the earth starting to have a slight vibration. He told the deck hands to disconnect the drill stem and close the blow out preventing valve. As they were closing the valve the noise was like a runaway freight train. Oil shot thru the half closed valve with a tremendous force. They got the valve closed, but were covered with oil. This well was a gusher.

At the end of the next week the well was flowing strong, pressure from inside the earth was forcing the oil into the large battery of tanks. Henry's faith paid off. As the Indians used to say, "He has strong medicine."

Wes Tex #1 was so strong that two tanker trucks could not keep the tanks from over flowing. Henry had two larger tank batteries set up and still the well had to be closed at times while the tanker trucks couldn't keep up. Henry told the company that was buying the oil to put more trucks on line or he would have to sell part of the oil to someone else. They added more trucks.

The pulling unit and the well were meeting all of the overhead and putting money in the bank. Wes Tex was on its way.

The deep hole rig had hit two dry holes in shallow sands, and the cost pulled hard on their pocket book. The fourth well they drilled was strong enough to recoup their losses, but it would take time. Oh well, you can't win them all.

Henry told his partners that if they hit on a fifty percent basis they would make more than they could spend. As time went by they were doing better than a sixty percent average.

James had hustled so much more work for the pulling unit that they were forced to purchase another. Phil had two crews on his hands.

Ruth was busy everyday keeping up with all of the paperwork that was being generated by the crews. Payroll was a weekly load that was taking up all day on Thursday. Wes Tex was a fast growing company.

Chapter Twenty Three

As the years slipped by Wes Tex had grown to a large company. It started with humble beginnings, and never had lost touch with them. Almost all of the employees were close friends of Henry's. Good people create good business.

Colonel Lee kept in touch, by mail, with James over the years. The last letter that James received told him that the war was in its last stages and should end soon. James knew that when it was over that the demand for oil would slow drastically. That meant that their business would slow down also.

James decided that he should talk to Henry about what was going to happen to the oil business in the near future. He asked Henry if they could have lunch together, that he needed to discuss an important matter with him.

After they had eaten, James told him of the last letter that he had received from Colonel Lee. "Well," Henry replied, "In a way that is real good news, but is also bad news for Wes Tex. What do you suggest we do?"

"Henry, I have received a few calls from the major players, asking if our business might be for sale. I told them that we might consider an offer, but that I must talk to my partners first. At the time I didn't even think about us selling. What do you think?"

"James, we got into this business to see if we could make enough money to have a good retirement. We have more money in the bank for the three of us to last two life times and have a good time doing it. We do not have any debt and we have some of the best equipment that money can buy. We also have the best crews in the state. We could close the door and walk away and leave it all and live a good life. If you think that we should sell, just get what you think the business is worth. Just be sure you sell all, everything, wells, leases and all. I'm ready to call it quits if you and Ruth are."

"I really think we should Henry. I would hate to see the bottom fall out of the market and the business would be worth next to nothing. I'll make a few calls and see if I can arouse some interest. I will talk with you and Ruth before I commit anything to anyone. I was just thinking that Simon might be the best way to approach a sale, as he has more contacts than anyone we know."

"If we offer that, sit on his can, brother of mine a commission he could sell real estate on the moon to people in China. Give him a call and get the ball rolling."

James placed a call to Simon that afternoon, telling him of their wanting to retire, and if he would be interested in handling the sale for them. Simon would be happy too. He would guarantee results at a price that the business was worth, and would charge them a commission of five percent. That fee would include all transfers of all real estate, wells, leases, tools and equipment. James told Simon that he would explain the deal to Ruth and Henry and call him back.

Henry told him that if he and Ruth approved of what Simon offered, to carry on.

"Henry, you put all of this business deal together when we first started, and Ruth and I will not take a three way split. You have put your heart and money into it and we cannot take two thirds of what you have built up."

"James, you have made the decisions that have covered all the risk that we have taken, and your foresight on what to do and when to do it and how to do it, have made us three millionaires three times over. Ruth has kept a perfect set of books and ran this office better than anyone could hope for. You two don't know how much you have helped me; I would have never made a go of it if it were not for you two. You both have earned your share, and I don't want to hear anymore about it." Henry could be hard headed when he wanted to.

After James and Ruth got home that afternoon, James told his dad that they had put the business up for sale.

"Well son, I think that it's the best thing that you all can do. I don't know how much money you have made, but it was the best thing that could have happened to and for you. The business gave you a goal to meet and you have no doubt had a good learning experience. I think now that you can handle your wounds without any problems. I know how much you miss working here on the ranch with me and the rest of the crew. You can do a lot more with your brains than you can chasing cows. How do Ruth and Henry feel about selling?"

"They think that with the war ending soon it's best to sell now while we can get what it's worth. I talked with Simon Fry, and he agreed to sell everything that we own, and handle all of the paper work for a five percent commission. Henry thinks that Simon probably already has someone lined up."

"What do you think Henry will do when the sale goes through?"

"I really don't know dad, Henry is one of the best men you could ask to be associated with. It has been a real pleasure working with him. I guess I had better try thinking of something to do when the business sells."

"Why don't you use a pickup instead of a horse, and take over some of the duties around here? I would like to have a little time to visit the twins, and do some fishing and get set up to go to Colorado, and check out our old hunting grounds. You can be a great help to me and Pepe. We are getting on in age and would like to bum around a little."

"There is nothing that I would like to do better than that. I just don't want you to think that I could not do the job right."

"James, you can handle any job better than anyone else, including me. You can take Ruth and Little Ben, and a have good time while you get this place back up to where it should be."

"I'll be ready to start the day the business is sold."

The next morning Simon called and wanted them to send him an inventory of all that was owned by Wes Tex. He also wanted a profit and loss statement for the past two years. Be sure to include any long and short term debts. Simon had a deal going already.

By noon, Ruth had all that Simon asked for in folders. All items were listed from the smallest tool to the largest drilling rig showing dates of purchase. She did not show any purchase prices. Photos of the real estate were included. Henry asked who was going to deliver them. They drew straws. Henry got the short one. James told him to take their car as his old truck was on its last leg. Henry agreed.

At the close of business on the last day of the month, Wes Tex was in the hands of the new owners. Henry, James and Ruth rented the community hall, and invited their entire crew and families to a catered barbecue to tell them how much they appreciated their loyalty and friendship. Henry explained that their jobs were secure; the only thing that would change would be the ownership. After the meal was finished, James handed Curtiss and Phil an envelope each and told them it was a little something extra for all that they had done for the company. Each received a bonus of ten thousand dollars, and a strong hand shake from Henry and James. Simon Fry banked a fair sum also. He made more money from his commission than he had ever made on a single transaction. Simon was happy.

Chapter Twenty Four

Joaquin took Pepe's job as El Segundo as James took over for his dad. Joaquin was never drafted, as his employment was more vital to the cause than serving in the military. Eva was happy about that. Maria was expecting their first child, and that made Eva happier. The cowboys knew the ranch and what needed to be accomplished as they were in the saddle with Pepe and Joaquin almost every day. The brush control crew was keeping the entire ranch free of the unwanted growth of undesirable plants. James and Joaquin kept a continuous watch on the fences as well as the numerous water wells for the live stock.

Life was good on the Adams ranch. James let Little Ben ride Peanut along with Joaquin on easy rides to check on the goats and sheep. The oil wells pumped day and night as Maude kept up with the books, and checked the production reports sent to her by Simon Fry. Only Maude and Ben knew how much money was piling up in Buddy's bank. It was a big pile.

One day James was by himself as he drove to the fields that were under the supervision of Slim Simmons.

It was almost lunch time, and James told Slim that he would like to take him to town and buy them lunch. Slim got in the pickup, and told James that he could not turn a deal like that down.

They ate the blue plate special at the Texas Cafe, and lingered over coffee.

James asked Slim how he ever got connected up with Ben.

"Well, some years back, my wife and I sold our place down close to Beeville and were looking for a place to buy. We loaded our few belongings and our two kids in a Model T Ford, and this is where we found a quarter section of good looking farm land, where we live now. It was four times the size of the place we sold and we fell in love with the place and the country here.

"Buddy Rose's daddy was running the bank back then, so I paid him a visit and he said that he would loan me the balance of the money that I needed to buy the place. My wife and I signed all of the papers and I started farming.

"The first two years we made good crops, and I paid what was due the bank for each year plus the interest. I managed to put away some money in case of trouble. The next year it come a hail storm and I lost everything that I had planted. I replanted, but it never rained a drop. My wife and I carried well water to our garden and what feed we needed for the mules, milk cow and the chickens. I had enough money to pay the years interest on my note but I told Mister Rose my problem and he told me maybe next year would be better. It wasn't. I planted and it never rained. Things were getting desperate. I was broke flatter than a flitter. My wife and I got down on our knees and asked the Good Lord for some help. The next day I went to the bank and told Mister Rose my problem again and that we prayed for the Lord's help.

"Mister Rose told me before I did anything else to go to the First Baptist Church and tell your problems to Brother Amos Brown. He is our preacher and he knows the way to God's heart. If anyone can get fast results its Amos. Don't you be bashful; you just do what Amos says and watch what happens.

"Well, I drove to the church and found Amos sweeping out the building. I introduced myself and told him that Mister Rose sent me to talk to him. I told him of our problem and our prayers. Amos asked me to kneel with him as he said a short prayer. I felt kinda' disappointed when he told me to go home and not to worry about a thing. He said that God knows your problem and will answer your prayers.

"The next morning we had cornbread with eggs and milk for breakfast, and I cranked up the old Tin Lizzy and was taking our two kids to school. I never felt so low in all my life.

"When I got back home there was a car parked in front of the house. I started up the porch steps when I smelled coffee. We hadn't had any coffee in the last two months. I couldn't figure for the life of me what was going on.

"When I walked into the kitchen there was a man and woman sitting at the table with Betty that I'd never seen before. The man got up and extended his hand, and asked if I was Slim Simmons. I could only nod my head. He told me that he was going to try to bribe me into doing some contract farming for him. I didn't know what to think or say. I glanced over at the kitchen counter and there were six large sacks of groceries setting there. His wife got up and helped Betty pour the coffee and place it on the table. I couldn't resist the coffee. After the first cup I finally found my voice and asked who they might be. He apologized for not introducing himself or his wife. Well James, it was your mom and dad.

"Ben told me that he was a cowboy and not a farmer and if he could farm from the back of a horse he might try farming but his horse won't go for it. He told me and the wife and kids to come out to the ranch and look over what he would want me to take care of. While we were looking, your mother and Betty could cook up supper. I told him we would be there after I picked the kids up from school.

"After I looked at the big irrigated fields I fell in love with the place. It was a farmer's paradise. Ben asked me how much it would cost him for me to take charge of all the farming with me hiring whatever help I might need. I scratched my head for a few seconds and gave him a price. He told me that I was short changing myself and told me that he would pay me twice as much and that I could use one of his tractors to work my place with. He gave me a hundred dollars in advance and told me to get to farming. I have been after it ever since. James I have never met a man as generous as your dad.

"On the way home I told Betty that we were going to start attending the church that Amos Brown was the pastor of. She told me that we were going to become members there. We did, the next Sunday."

The Lord and Amos work in strange and mysterious ways.

The year passed and one day there was jubilation in America. The war in Europe was at an end at last. The next few months went quickly and Japan decided that the atomic bombs were more than they could handle, and they called it quits also. The world was at peace again. Thank the Lord.

The American industries did an about face, and started making things for use in life instead of destruction. Automobiles, tractors, washing machines, and baby beds rolled off of the assembly lines instead of tanks, planes, guns, and ships. Peace was a wonderful thing.

Ben and Pepe loaded up the horses and their gear and headed for a few weeks' vacation in the mountains. Things were getting back to normal.

James, Ruth, Maude and Little Ben were sitting on the front porch late one afternoon, when a new red pickup pulled up and stopped. Maude asked, "Now who in the world can that be? Oh my, that's Henry. I look a fright awful. Tell him I'm putting on some coffee, and I'll try to spruce up a little before he sees me looking like this." She completed the task in record time.

Henry was dressed like he was going courting. Maybe he was.

It was good to see Henry; he seemed like one of the family. He always had a positive attitude and good smile;

you couldn't help but like him.

Maude asked, "Henry, what are you up to now days? We haven't seen you for a month of Sundays, and here you are driving a new truck, and all dressed up like you are fixing to go to church."

"Well, I've decided to turn over a new leaf in my life. I thought I'd come out and see if you would accompany me to having supper in Angelo and take in a movie. I know that I should call first, but it would be easy for you to say no over the phone. So here I am."

"Henry, I haven't been to a movie in years and I think I would enjoy your company. Let me freshen up a bit and I'll be ready."

After they left Ruth told James, "Well, I guess Maude will be leaving us soon. Did you see her light up when Henry drove up? She has asked me several times if he was still around."

The week after Ben and Pepe got back from the mountains, Amos Brown married Maude and Henry on the front porch of the ranch house. It was a simple ceremony, just like they wanted it to be.

Little Ben was growing up, like all children do. He saddled his own horse and rode where he wanted to. He was with Ben most of the time, getting an education on how to be a rancher. There was not a better place for a man to be, riding a good horse and working cattle.

Joaquin and Maria had a son and a daughter now, and Eva was in an earthly heaven.

Grandchildren make grandparents happy.

Ben made a trip to see Simon Fry, and handed him a hand written folder.

"Simon, this is a will that I have written in just plain English. I want you to put it in lawyer words and get it recorded for me. Just make sure that the two sections of land that I have that are on the North West corner are deeded to the Rojas family with the two oil wells and mineral rights, along with the live stock I have listed."

The lawyer looked the will over, and told Ben that he was being awful generous.

"Simon, I have never seen a rental truck or an armored car at the cemetery. I only know of one person who wanted to be buried with a pocket knife. I can't take any earthly thing with me, but I can help someone else enjoy it."

On his way home Ben stopped in Eden and called Amos. "Hey old friend, if you don't have any plans, I'll pick you up in about an hour and buy your supper."

"I'll be ready Ben. You know good and well that I can't cook worth a hoot."

Ben hadn't seen much of Amos the past few weeks, as he and Pepe's trip kept him from church as well as the week he spent with the twins. He missed visiting with Amos and enjoyed his sense of humor.

They ate at the cafeteria, where Amos had a larger variety of the food he enjoyed most. After the meal was finished, and they were enjoying another cup of coffee, Amos told Ben that he missed him in church, but he knew that a man needed a time to relax.

"Amos, have you ever wanted to take a long trip, and see something that you always dreamed about?"

"Ben, I have always wanted to go and see the Holy Land. I have pictured so much in my mind, as I read the Bible, that I would just like to see if things and places are anything like what I see in my thoughts. I truly think that would be the trip of a lifetime."

On his way to the ranch, Ben thought how would be the best way to send Amos on his dream trip. A travel agency should know. There was one in Angelo across the street from Buddy's bank. Ben was there when they opened the door.

Ben told the young lady that he wanted the best and longest trip to the Holy Land that she could book as quickly as possible. She handed Ben a travel guide and told him to look at what was offered by that company while she tried another. Most of the trips were for two weeks. If you went by ship most of the time was spent at sea. Ben knew that Amos did not like to fly so he must figure a way to make the trip last long enough for Amos to see all that was possible.

"Sir, here is something that might interest you. There is a church group that offers a place to stay as long as you want, with all meals, guide service, and transportation furnished. It suggests that to see all the recommend tour in detail that you should book at least sixty days. They even take you to Egypt and Greece."

"Young lady, could you tell me where you leave from by ocean liner to get there the closest from here?"

"Let me look in another book that has port of calls in that area and where they depart from. There is one that departs from Houston next week and it is a two week trip with a stop in Miami for a day's lay over. It is a first class only liner with the best suites and food available. It is a little expensive but that is all I can find."

"How soon can you have all the arrangements made?"

"I can have everything ready for you by noon. It will require a deposit in order to save you a berth on the liner."

"Tell me how much the round trip and the complete tour will be for the sixty days."

The lady got the adding machine going and told Ben it would cost him four-thousand-two-hundred-seventy-dollars and thirty six cents. Ben wrote out a check and told her to make out the reservations for Reverend Amos Brown. He thanked the lady and told her he would be back after lunch.

That afternoon he called the three deacons of the church and requested a meeting at the close of business at Buddy's bank. Slim, Buddy and Earl were the deacons, so Ben would be in good company.

Ben explained all that Amos said about how he would like to make this trip, so he was going to send him.

"I think that this is a wonderful thing you are doing Ben." Earl said," But we have one problem, you all know that Amos will not leave the church without a replacement."

Slim spoke up, "Well, we can fire him until he returns, and we can use the four weeks trial preachers like we did when Amos had that stroke."

Buddy said "Let's do it." They did.

Ben and Slim drove Amos to Houston to make sure he didn't miss the ship. They helped him to his cabin and wished him a good voyage and to enjoy the tour. Ben handed Amos a thirty five mm camera and two dozen rolls of color film. He also handed him a sealed envelope with two thousand dollars in it and told him not to open it until he was out of port. Slim and Ben waited on the dock as the gang plank was raised, and waved goodbye to their old friend.

Chapter Twenty Five

Amos returned from his extended trip, and resumed his duties at the church. He had all of the photos that he had taken made into slides. He had purchased a projector and screen. The first Sunday night that he was back, the regular service was dismissed and the slide show began. Amos had eight hundred and sixty four slides and planned to show seventy two slides every month to the members. This would take a year to complete the tour. It was an event that boosted the attendance on every fourth Sunday night service.

Ben, Earl, and Buddy made their fall hunting trip to Colorado each year as it was time for the older folks to enjoy the fruits of their labors. Could you blame them?

Ruth had taken over the bookkeeping from Maude as Henry was taking her on an extended vacation in the Caribbean. Maude made sure that Ruth learned how to make sourdough biscuits and keep the starter alive before they left. Maude purchased herself a bathing suit and made Henry get one too. Henry couldn't swim.

Time passes and the older you become the years pass faster. Seasons come and go so fast you think you should just pull a cotton sack over the Christmas tree and let it stand in the corner with the lights off.

The old saying, To Soon Old, To Late Smart, still applies to most folks. Well, life is just doing the best you can with what you've got.

Should you happen by the Adams ranch today you might see James and Ruth sitting on the front porch rocking their great grandson.

Little Ben would be in the corral breaking a blue roan horse that he had named Percy Two. His son would be punching cows with Joaquin's son somewhere on the ranch.

Slim's grandson would be driving a new tractor,

planting the fields to grow crops for the fall harvest.

There would be a few more headstones in the family cemetery and the native Texas wild flowers in all their glory would be covering the good earth.

Life still goes on and the best people in the world still live in West Texas.

The End

Made in the USA
San Bernardino, CA
02 May 2017